RAILROAD RANGERS

To forget an unhappy past, lawyer Gerald Gower left his job in New York to start a new life working for the Union Pacific Railroad. But having the tough, unpredictable Lieutenant Liam O'Neill for a colleague only made Gower's introduction to the harsh western way of life that much more difficult. O'Neill held Gower and his soft city ways in contempt, and Gower was tested beyond endurance. The sparks would surely fly!

TERRY MURPHY

RAILROAD RANGERS

Complete and Unabridged

LINFORD
Leicester

First published in Great Britain in 2001 by
Robert Hale Limited
London

First Linford Edition
published 2003
by arrangement with
Robert Hale Limited
London

British Library CIP Data

Murphy, Terry, *1962 –*
    Railroad rangers.—Large print ed.—
Linford western library
    1. Western stories
    2. Large type books
    I. Title
    823.9'14 [F]

    ISBN 0–7089–4913–4

Published by
F. A. Thorpe (Publishing)
Anstey, Leicestershire

Set by Words & Graphics Ltd.
Anstey, Leicestershire
Printed and bound in Great Britain by
T. J. International Ltd., Padstow, Cornwall

1

Facing a fierce judge in a courtroom
had never been as daunting as this. The
building was not large by New York
standards, but it intimidated Gerald
Gower. He hesitated, wondering if his
sense of adventure had led him astray?
A Broadway car passed by, its two
plodding horses as bored-looking as the
passengers who stared unseeingly out at
Gower. It was a reminder of the
monotony of city life from which he
planned to escape. A man needed space
around him, otherwise he felt
oppressed, defeated, and spent his life
bogged down worrying over trivial
things. There was no way a widower at
the young age of 30 could begin a new
life in the too-familiar surroundings of
New York. Yet he doubted that as a
successful hometown lawyer he could
function in the wilderness out West. He

was fit, strong and tough, but was that enough? There had to be something insolubly contradictory in the premise of practising law in a savage land. His enthusiasm ebbed. Already gone was his delight at being chosen from more than a score of applicants.

Maybe he was mistaken, and the less forbidding office block next door was the building he sought. He checked the address: 20 Nassau Street. This was the right place. Further confirmation came from the fascia board above the double doors, which read THE UNION PACIFIC RAILWAY COMPANY.

Squaring his shoulders, Gower mounted the wide concrete steps and entered the building. An uninterested doorman didn't even reply to his announcement that he was there to see Colonel Silas Seymour. The aloof man beckoned a lad who was dressed similarly to a bellhop at the new and swanky Fifth Avenue Hotel on Twenty-third Street. The young flunky led Gower up two flights of majestic stairs to the second floor and along a thickly carpeted landing. He was ushered into an office that was heavy with the smell of pipe tobacco.

A tall, elderly man rose up from behind a huge antique desk. A thick grey moustache curled up at the ends gave a false impression of smiling as he stretched out a hand. 'Ah, Gower, how good of you to call on us. I have anticipated our meeting with pleasure. You come highly recommended. I am Silas Seymour, retired colonel and the Union Pacific's consulting engineer.'

'It's good to meet you, sir,' Gower said, shaking the colonel's hand. It pleased him to notice a copy of the recently issued Wiley & Putman book *Tales by Edgar A. Poe* on the desk. Gower had feared that by accepting a new job he was joining up with the unread, the uneducated.

There was a third person in the room. A man of about Gower's age was standing looking out of a window. Remaining with his back to them, he was clad in fringed buckskin and had fair hair that was worn long. The man made an incongruous figure in a city where even the down-and-outs in the Bowery were clad in what once were smart suits. From illustrations seen in cheap and trashy publications about the Wild West, Gower put the man down as an army scout. He was trying to solve the riddle of how an army scout came to be in a plush New York office, when Seymour interrupted his thoughts by inviting him to be seated.

In a high-backed chair, the colonel rested his elbows on his desk, balancing his chin on steepled fingers. His unusually pale-blue eyes held Gower in an unwavering gaze. 'This business of interviewing is a little out of my field, Gower, but the company has asked me to meet you. I will try to answer any questions you may have. Is there anything specific that you wish to ask?'

'Nothing specific, sir, but I would welcome a general outline of what will be expected of me. I have no idea what my duties will be.'

'Oh dear,' Seymour sighed with a frown. 'I am not the man most suited to this task. However, I will do what I can. You will be conversant with the fact that the Union Pacific Railway Company board is currently engaged in building a great national railroad. From Omaha it goes west and will extend nearly sixteen hundred miles from the Missouri River, across the Great Plains and over the largely unexplored Rocky Mountain Ranges. It will continue from Salt Lake down the Humboldt Valley to pass over and through the massive Sierra Nevadas. It will reach the Pacific slope within a hundred miles of Sacramento, Gower.'

'I have read about this inspiring project, sir,' Gower acknowledged. 'That is why I wanted to become a part of it.'

'The company is grateful that an esteemed lawyer such as yourself is willing to provide us with your valued services, Gower. But I have been asked to acquaint you with the considerable dangers you will be facing.'

The man at the window had remained immobile. But Gower sensed that he was listening intently to the conversation. The colonel's warning puzzled Gower. The topographical parties determining the route ahead of the railroad had suffered many deaths from attacks by hostile Indians and the elements. But as a lawyer, he would have no place among these surveyors. He told the colonel, 'I don't understand, sir.'

Seymour said sympathetically, 'I should give you some background. You see, the vast scale of our endeavour means that we are unlike any ordinary industry. The Union Pacific's railway builders' advance across the continent is best described as that of a great army. But though we have the protection of the United States Army, we are not an army, Gower. We are not granted the latitude that an army enjoys, and rightly so, of course. However, just as it is

6

necessary for us to move forward at speed, so is it just as necessary that we do so peaceably. You will ensure that the company is within the law at all times, Gower.'

'I have followed you so far, Colonel.'

'The problem is, Gower, that we are rapidly nearing land on which farmers have been allowed to settle. Those farmers have provided irrigation and have cultivated what was virtually a desert.'

Gower pre-empted Seymour. 'And the Union Pacific Railway Company now wants that land.'

'Not *wants*, Gower; the company is *entitled* to the land. The Government has granted the land in question to the Union Pacific Railway Company.'

'With respect, sir,' Gower began, 'I doubt that the farmers who have devoted their lives to that land, who have laboured from dawn to dusk, will accept that the company is entitled to it.'

'Exactly. Which is why you are likely

to find yourself between two hostile forces. It is anticipated that the farmers will offer violence, and bands of Sioux Indians are active in that territory. Make no mistake about it, son, you'll earn your money. Initially, you will visit each farm in turn. You will explain how the farmer stands in law and, if necessary, negotiate.'

'What leeway will I have when negotiating, sir?'

'The company holds the winning hand, Gower, so your powers of negotiation will be very limited,' Seymour answered. 'You will have to ensure that you make no concessions. We are not talking about illiterate nesters. You will encounter some hothead farmers blasting away with shotguns, but we have been reliably informed that the majority have united to resist us legally. They will be taking the Union Pacific to court, Gower, and we know that you are the best man to deal with that situation. You will be escorted at all times,' Colonel Seymour assured him, turning his head to the man at the window, who slowly brought himself round to face into the room.

Gower saw that the man was handsome, his facial features more refined than suggested by his style of dress. He had the poise and sophistication of a gentleman, together with the menace of a savage. Gower had the impression that the man might shake him by the hand or slit his throat. Either of the two options would come easily to the fair-haired man.

'This is Lieutenant Liam O'Neill of the United States Army,' the colonel said stiffly. 'He is a somewhat unconventional but nevertheless, excellent soldier. As a former senior officer, I abhor the first trait, but admire the second attribute. Lieutenant O'Neill will take the train to Omaha with you in the morning. When you move west from there, Lieutenant O'Neill and his troop will ensure that you are under full protection at all times.'

'With luck, Gower,' O'Neill said, in a

voice so low-pitched that it was just audible, 'the only redskin you'll see will be one we've killed. You look to me like you've been a city man all your life, mister; am I right?'

'That's correct,' Gower nodded. 'New York born and bred.'

'Hardly the right training for where you're heading, Gower.'

'It's Mr Gower's legal training that interests the company,' Seymour pointed out.

'I appreciate that, Colonel,' O'Neill drawled. 'But a lawyer's document is no protection against a bullet from a Henry rifle, and a Sioux buck with blood in his eye sure won't be stopped with a legal writ.'

'You will be between that Sioux buck and Gower, O'Neill. That is your assignment.'

Without looking at Seymour, O'Neill said, 'It isn't possible to give protection at all times in combat. Things get confused in a fight, Colonel.'

'I don't need you to tell me what it's

like in a fight Lieutenant,' Seymour said testily.

'I guess not,' O'Neill responded, with a disrespectful shrug. He changed his attitude and the subject. 'Tell me, are you a drinking man, Gower?'

'I take a drink to be sociable.'

'Then I hope that you're feeling sociable right now,' O'Neill said, 'so's you can show me round this big city of yours.'

Aware that Colonel Seymour was awaiting his answer with interest, Gower wanted to reject O'Neill's suggestion. It would suit him fine not to see this belligerent soldier again until they met at the railway station in the morning. A quiet evening would suit him, his last chance to visit Lola's grave in a lonely little spot in the hillside at the Cypress Hills Cemetery. He tried to conjure up an excuse. Saying that he had much to do on his last night at home wouldn't work. Selling up their house when Lola had died, he had moved into lodgings at Bleeker Street.

The address was on his application that now lay on the colonel's desk.

Irritated by Gower's hesitation, the colonel spoke up. 'I'd look on it right kindly, Gower, if you took care of the lieutenant, a stranger in town, tonight.'

'Of course,' Gower replied grudgingly, wondering if it was an ill omen that his first duty for the United Pacific Railway Company was one that he had no liking for.

'Welcome to the company,' the colonel said as he stood to shake hands vigorously. He seemed immensely relieved to have passed O'Neill over to Gower's care. That had to mean that the lieutenant couldn't be trusted alone in New York.

Liam O'Neill rammed a battered Stetson on his fair-haired head and moved to the door. 'Lead the way, Gower. I'm as dry as a Death Valley gopher.'

Out on the street, Gower was keenly aware of the curious stares directed at the oddly dressed man at his side.

O'Neill had a smooth, graceful walk, and an appearance of total relaxation, but Gower sensed that beneath the calm exterior, the soldier was as edgy and watchful as a feeding bird. O'Neill seemed to expect an attack to come from every corner they approached, every alleyway they passed.

On Fourteenth Street the New York Circus had just opened for a short season. The billboard outside still announced that the circus featured 'The Wonderful Cynocephalus — the Most Unique of Novelties'. Lola and himself had many times laughingly speculated on what this might be. Now she would never know.

O'Neill interrupted his sad thoughts by pointing to a building opposite the circus, and asking, 'What's that place?'

'The Academy of Music.'

'I don't reckon as how they'll be playing the kind of tunes in there that I want to hear tonight,' the lieutenant observed. 'What have you got in mind, Gower?'

All that Gerald Gower had in mind was a need to somehow get away from O'Neill. He lamely offered, 'There's the Strand and the Idlewild on Sixth Avenue.'

'Saloons?'

'Yes.'

'Any difference between the two, Gower?'

'If there is, I've never noticed,' Gower replied.

'Then we'll take the nearest one,' O'Neill said with a solemn nod.

That was the Idelwild. By walking a few blocks they entered a different world, a world considerably lower in tone than the one they had just left. A bar was immediately inside of the door, and a long room at the rear was dotted with beer-wet tables. The room was packed with men and women all in various stages of intoxication. A young man at the piano was playing 'Listen to the Mocking Bird'.

As Gower and O'Neill passed through the chattering throng, they had

14

to step over a drunken woman who was lying on the floor. A fight broke out further into the room, and there was much swearing and the breaking of glass. No one seemed alarmed. Without being asked, a passing girl with a heavily painted face informed them, 'That's just Ikey Heenan punching Yankee Welch's head. Don't let it worry you.'

'It doesn't worry me,' O'Neill said.

The girl took a closer look at him, squinting. 'What are you, some kind of cowboy?'

'No, ma'am, a buffalo hunter,' O'Neill replied gravely.

'Good hunting,' the girl said with a smile, as she deftly rolled a cigarette.

'This is sure some groggery, Gower. I'm going to wake snakes here tonight,' O'Neill said, as he looked around appreciatively.

Knowing enough Western slang to understand that the untamed O'Neill intended to cause a ruckus once he'd had a few drinks, Gower didn't want to be involved. They were at the bar ordering whiskey that O'Neill referred to as 'tarantula juice'. Tobacco smoke floated lazily over the suffocating room. There were a thousand places where Gerald Gower would have preferred to be.

The young man at the piano was singing 'Dixie's Land' in a surprisingly good voice. The girl from before came to them, the cigarette alight and dangling from her lips. She made a show of looking round her, before remarking to O'Neill, 'The buffalo seem thin on the ground.'

'It's real early yet. I'll need you later to help me skin the creatures, miss.' O'Neill downed his drink in one. 'What'll you have?'

'Get me a beer.' The girl, who could not be more than seventeen, leaned nonchalantly on the bar close to O'Neill.

Gower didn't want to be there. Though Lola was dead and gone, he felt that he was letting her down by just being in this bawdyhouse. He shook his head as O'Neill gestured for him to empty his glass. This was still Gower's first drink, and he was determined that it would be his only one. He shuddered inwardly as he saw O'Neill's head tilt back to finish his third whiskey in quick succession. Never had Gower seen a man so intent on trouble as this strangely dressed, long-haired soldier.

'Take it easy, O'Neill,' he advised. 'We should get a good night's sleep ready for the journey to Omaha tomorrow.'

Tossing coins on the counter for more drinks for him and the girl, O'Neill retorted, 'No one's keeping you here, Gower. This is my night to howl. Tomorrow I have to go back to being a soldier; giving orders, taking orders, salutin' with a back as stiff as an eighteen-inch bayonet.'

Accepting that he couldn't dislodge O'Neill from the Idlewild, Gower felt obliged to stay. It would be disastrous to later let a drunken O'Neill loose alone to roam about the crime-ridden streets and alleys of New York. Anything serious happening to O'Neill would mean that Gower's career with the Union Pacific Railway Company would end before it had begun.

Time passed, with Gower enduring 'darky' songs, with the clatter of bones and thump of the tambourine of a minstrel band. The players were genuine from Sullivan and Thompson Streets, and were paid in beer.

The trouble anticipated by Gower came when the girl was waiting for a beer, which would be her tenth since joining O'Neill. The first warning was the sudden hush that fell on the assembly. Then two policemen approached the girl who was with O'Neill. More officers had come into the saloon to line up along the full of one wall. The two policeman asked, 'Judith Hill?'

The expression of fright on the face of the girl, which had too much rouge upon the cheek and too much powder shading it was enough confirmation for the officers. One grabbed her arm. 'Come with us, please.'

O'Neill had started to protest when another man, the ruffian type, walked over and squared up aggressively to the two policemen. He was a huge fellow who dwarfed the law officers, both of whom must have stood over six feet. 'Take your hands off the girl. She's a friend of mine.'

Seeing this man as his principal enemy for some peculiar reason, the half-drunken O'Neill, despite the other fellow being something like twice his size, felled him with one lightning punch. Releasing the girl, the two policemen made a grab for O'Neill, but he sent them both flying with accurately delivered punches. Blood splattered freely from the smashed nose of one policeman, while the jaw of his colleague had been unhinged so that it was out of line with the rest of his face. Then there was pandemonium as the line of police officers moved forwards.

Ready for them, O'Neill went fighting mad. Others in the saloon surged forwards to help him, but they were driven back by a line of police.

Keeping clear of the mêlée, Gower saw the girl flee unnoticed as policeman after policeman fell under O'Neill's frenzied assault. O'Neill was cheered on but, at last, the police got the better of him. A burly officer caught him a heavy blow high up on the face. As O'Neill reeled, momentarily stunned, another policeman swung a nightstick that clunked dully against O'Neill's skull and he fell face downwards to the floor.

Policemen pounced on O'Neill, delivering a few swift kicks to his inert body. Moving in as policemen dragged an unconscious O'Neil to his feet, Gower came face to face with Captain Byrne. They normally came together only in the city's courtrooms.

The police captain's face registered his shock. 'Mr Gower! I didn't expect to find you in a place like this.'

'I'm here on business, Captain

Byrne,' Gower explained. He nodded at O'Neill, who, head resting on his chest, was being supported by police officers. 'That man is a lieutenant in the United States Army.'

'Beggin' your pardon, Mr Gower, are you sure?' the police chief frowned. 'He doesn't fit my picture of an army officer.'

'I agree that he doesn't look the part, Captain Byrne,' Gower replied dourly, 'but I can assure you that Lieutenant Liam O'Neill is an officer, though maybe not a gentleman in the present circumstances.'

Four policemen were carrying O'Neill bodily towards the door of the saloon. The big man O'Neill had knocked out was also under arrest. Handcuffed to an officer, he made his way unsteadily to the exit.

'Just a temporary lapse, most likely,' the captain remarked.

'I hope so, but I doubt it Captain Byrne,' Gower said cynically. 'But you can have your men put him down. He is in my charge. I'll take him off your hands.'

'Now that's real difficult, Mr Gower,' an embarrassed Byrne mumbled, revealing a receding hairline by pushing back his silver-decorated hat. 'He's under arrest.'

'Release O'Neill, Captain, and I'll sign anything you need to absolve you from duty where he is concerned.'

'I'm afraid not, Mr Gower,' Byrne said apologetically. 'You can collect him in the morning from the Fifteenth Precinct.'

2

They had left Omaha at ten o'clock that morning, in a train made up for excursionists with elegant, comfortable carriages. It was a vast improvement on the journey from New York. The day on which he had left home had begun badly. Captain Byrne had been reluctant to release Liam O'Neill. In a disorderly state brought about by drinking and fighting, O'Neill looked as if he belonged among the ruffians with whom he had shared a barred cage. No one would have believed from his appearance that he was a military officer. There was nothing about him that even hinted that he was worth rescuing from jail. Though silently agreeing that the police had every right to retain O'Neill and have him stand trial, Gower had argued successfully that the army lieutenant be released. An ungrateful, surly O'Neill had hardly uttered a word to Gower from New York to Omaha. Seated in a corner, O'Neill had occasionally and tenderly fingered the long blue and black swelling that began just above his right eye and disappeared into his hairline. It was a reminder of where the policeman's stick had cracked O'Neill across the head in the Idlewild. Though unsympathetic, Gower accepted that the residual pain from the blow, combined with the after effects of alcohol, was causing O'Neill considerable distress.

O'Neill must have been feeling better since leaving Omaha. Though he now sat with his Stetson tilted over his face, apparently asleep, he had earlier been slightly more communicative. Apart from finding it impossible to like the army lieutenant, Gower had no need of companionship right then. Everything about the scenery they were passing through filled him with wonder. The track stretching ahead was leading to a distant valley. He estimated that the low, rolling hills to the north were twenty miles away, and the opposite and similar range to the south were at the same distance. The hills sank into the plains to create perfect horizons on both sides of the train.

The splendid green ocean in between was something that a city man such as Gower could never find words to describe. For the first time since the death of his wife, Gower felt a stirring of interest in life. Maybe the vast change and the challenge presented by his new job would ease his pain and grief, but nothing could ever fill his sense of loss. O'Neill spoke from under his hat, referring to the view from the carriage window without needing to see it.

'The Mormon Trail north of the Platte,' he said, identifying the scene that held Gower in awe. 'A different world to that of New York, eh, Gower?'

'It certainly is,' Gower half sighed in agreement. Right then he felt that he was between two worlds, with a longing for the familiar one of New York and an urge for the new world beckoning across the vast plains.

Across the aisle from them, a mother and father smiled fondly at their two children, a boy and a girl, as they squealed with delight at each new marvel they spotted. Gower felt ashamed of his own childishness that filled him with an excitement equal to that of the boy.

Amazed at how level the ground was, he remarked to O'Neill, 'The surface is perfectly flat for almost as far as the eye can see.'

With his Stetson still covering his face, O'Neill put him right on this. 'Though it may seem flat, Gower, the ground rises a regular ten feet to the mile as we head west. That makes for ample drainage. The soil is very rich.'

This made Gower realize that there was more to O'Neill than the buckskin-clad hell-raiser he had been in New

York. The soldier wasn't trying to impress with his knowledge of the territory, but spoke of the terrain with a kind of reverence. They were nearing the mouth of the valley and much of the land was under cultivation. Teams of eight oxen created furrows of deep, black, freshly turned loam as slowly they drew along huge ploughs. This earthy blackness contrasted with the dark green of wheat and the lighter shades of grass to produce a colourful mosaic.

'Don't let yourself get carried away with how peaceful it all looks, Gower.'

The sound of O'Neill's voice brought Gower out of what he recognized as having been largely a pleasant daydream. He turned to find that the officer had pushed his Stetson back up on his head and was studying him. Gower found it difficult to equate O'Neill's delicately handsome features with the man of extreme violence that he knew him to be.

'This is something that a man like me

will take a time to get used to, O'Neill,' he admitted.

'Don't worry,' O'Neill advised as he stretched lazily. 'You'll get used to it real quick the first time Red Cloud and his Sioux warriors come sweeping over a hill at you.'

As O'Neill stood, the boy across from them looked at him admiringly. Gower realized that the buckskin-clad figure was to the lad one of the Wild West heroes he had read about. Gower wondered how many of the others were flawed knights of the frontier? O'Neill was probably, a brave and efficient soldier; Gower had no way of knowing, but as a civilized human being he was sorely lacking.

As the train followed a modest bend, O'Neill pointed ahead. 'We're about to cross the North Platte. That bridge you see is some three thousand feet long. We'll soon be at North Platte Station, where we'll be staying overnight.'

'What sort of a place is it?' Gower enquired, wondering if he was going to have to rough it this early in the trip West.

'When I came through here last Fall there wasn't one building in North Platte,' O'Neill replied as he reached for his war bag. 'Now the Union Pacific has fine brick carriage houses, and fronting the track are thirty-six buildings, including a hotel that does good grub. The company will pick up the tab for one night. Make the most of it Gower, for it could well be your last night with a roof over your head.'

This reminder of what was ahead caused Gower some consternation. Then he had further misgivings as he watched O'Neill take from his bag a holstered six-shooter wrapped in a gunbelt. Unrolling the belt O'Neill buckled it round his waist, then stooped to tie a thong from the holster round his thigh. It seemed that somehow the gunbelt emphasized the width of O'Neill's shoulders and the leanness of his hips.

A worried Gower warned him, 'If you

intend seeking trouble in North Platte, O'Neill, I want no part in it. I prefer to stick to the civilized life that I'm used to.'

'You got it wrong,' O'Neill said with a slow shake of his head. He patted the handle of the holstered gun. 'This is for protection. In the past with my troop and in the line of duty, I've done things that no man should ever do to people. There's a lot of men out there, Gower, and possibly a few women, who would gun me down without a second thought if they came across me out of uniform and all alone.'

Though he gave what O'Neill said a lot of thought, Gower reserved comment until they had booked rooms in an unexpectedly luxurious hotel. When they had descended the stairs to take a table in the low-ceilinged restaurant that occupied the entire front of the hotel, Gower followed up on what O'Neill had said.

'The reason you gave for wearing a gun, O'Neill,' Gower said, to get back to the subject. 'You never struck me as a man likely to be much troubled by his conscience.'

'I imagine that you in your work, just the same as me doing my job, Gower, you can only permit yourself so much conscience.'

In his head, Gower conceded that this was true in part. After several successful defences in court, he had been troubled by the conviction that he had been instrumental in having a guilty person escape punishment. But his line of work was very different to that of O'Neill, and he pointed this out.

'I suppose you're right in a way, O'Neill, but I wouldn't agree that the people I have influence over suffer as severely as the unfortunate folk you deal with.'

'For an educated professional man, Gower, you show a lack of horse sense,' O'Neill said, conversationally rather than critically. 'Surely what we are discussing here is not what we do to our victims, but how our actions affect us personally.'

Staggered by O'Neill's erudition and high intellect, Gower was temporarily lost for words. To fill the gap in conversation, he said, 'I find you a difficult man to get to know, O'Neill.'

'Make it easy on yourself by not trying,' O'Neill advised in his mild-voiced manner. 'The railroad has brought you and me together, Gower. If that weren't so, we wouldn't even walk on the same side of the street.'

That was very true. Gower would never have mixed with anyone of O'Neill's kind in normal life. Nevertheless he considered that, as they had to work together, some sort of relationship should be established between them. They could never be friends because they had nothing in common, but some rules of behaviour toward each other needed to be established.

'I accept that, O'Neill. But we are together, so surely a degree of mutual respect would benefit us both?'

With a brief, mirthless grin, O'Neill said, 'I'm not the sort of man a city-dweller like yourself could respect Gower, and you would have to earn my respect which is something I can't ever see happening.'

The insult in this cold rebuff hurt Gower. He was preparing to remonstrate with O'Neill when a middle-aged man walked up to their table. Like Gower, he was dressed in the garb of an Easterner. The yellow light of oil lamps disclosed a stern, hawk-nosed face and steel-grey hair that gave him a commanding presence. The man's appearance was so impressive that Gower almost missed the young woman who stood a little behind him. She was a slender brunette in her early twenties, with an attractive, strong-featured face. Noticing how certain angles of the lamplight brought out the coppery twinkles of her hair, Gower was suddenly shocked to find himself looking at a woman for the first time since Lola had died. He hastily searched for the wife he carried in his heart and remembered in his dreams.

Both O'Neill and he stood up from the table. Shaking hands with the man, O'Neill turned to Gower. 'Meet Mr Samuel Glendon of the Union Pacific Railway Company, Gower. Mr Glendon, this is Gerald Gower, the lawyer whom Colonel Seymour engaged in New York.'

'Mr Gower.' Glendon shook Gower's hand warmly. 'Silas speaks highly of you, and I must say that you have the cut of the kind of man our railroad likes. Please, meet my daughter, Mercedes.'

'I'm pleased to meet you, Mr Gower,' the girl said, as Gower took her slim, cool hand.

Her deep-brown eyes hid more of her than they revealed, imparting a mystique that gripped Gower. Resembling her father, with a firm jawline such as Glendon probably possessed as a younger man, the girl had a beauty that was all the more compelling because it was indefinable. The observant Gower noticed that though she hadn't spoken to O'Neill, the two of them had exchanged a quick, almost furtive glance. He wondered what that meant.

'I must permit you gentlemen to continue with your meal. We are in company for dinner,' Samuel Glendon said apologetically.

'It was good of you to make yourself known to us, sir,' O'Neill said.

'I confess that I had an ulterior motive in approaching you, Lieutenant O'Neill.' Glendon's heavy brows contracted until they met above the hawk-like beak of a nose. 'As you are still on your New York assignment, and especially as you have no troops under your command here, I have no right to ask this of you.'

'Ask away, Mr Glendon,' O'Neill volunteered.

O'Neill's response and his general manner toward Glendon made Gower see the army lieutenant from a new angle. With an eye to when he would leave the army, O'Neill was preparing a preliminary base for an eventual career with the Union Pacific Railway Company.

'We are losing stores every night, in large quantities, here in Omaha, Lieutenant O'Neill. The box cars in the freight yard are being robbed, and we don't have enough men to guard them.'

'I'll look into it tonight sir,' O'Neill promised.

'This will have to be unofficial, Lieutenant,' Glendon stressed.

'It will be sir, and it will be effective.'

Glendon shook hands with both of them again. 'I know that I can rely on you, Lieutenant O'Neill. Now, Mercedes and I must return to our people. It was a pleasure meeting you, Mr Gower.'

Acknowledging this with a little bow that he shared between father and daughter, Gower received a curt nod in exchange from Mercedes Glendon. There was some kind of fleeting exchange between the girl and O'Neill, and the Glendons then walked away.

As O'Neill hurriedly finished what remained of an excellent meal, he suggested, 'You turn in early, Gower, and I'll meet up with you in the morning. I've this business of Mr Glendon's to attend to.'

'I'd like to go along with you, O'Neill,' Gower said tentatively. 'If my job is going to be as rough as you say, I might as well get used to it early on.'

O'Neill frowned at him. 'I can't stop you if you want to join me, but do you know what you're letting yourself in for? I'm not going out in the night to shuffle papers around on an office desk. Can you handle a gun?'

'I've never fired a handgun, but I belonged to a club in New York and did quite a bit of rifle shooting.'

'That's a help,' O'Neill acknowledged, 'but I don't know if it will be enough. I think I know who is taking stuff from the railroad. If I'm right, then it's a gang of Union Army men who deserted during the war. They are a rough and tough bunch, Gower.'

'I've never been afraid to face anything, O'Neill.'

Considering this for a few moments, O'Neill then gave a decisive nod. 'Wait for me out on the hotel steps.'

Gower was waiting for a quarter of an hour out in a blue/black night before O'Neill came to him. The lieutenant was again wearing his gunbelt with its tied-down holster. He carried a rifle which he tossed to Gower, watching intently and seemingly relieved when Gower deftly caught the weapon.

'I've got us a couple of horses waiting in case we need them,' O'Neill said. 'But we'll go on foot first.'

'Where are we going?'

'To the nearest hobo camp. They won't be into this kind of large scale thieving, but they know what's going on around here.'

The shrill blasts of a train whistling in the distance came to them as they moved off. Gower couldn't match the way O'Neill moved silently and swiftly through the night. When they had passed a water-tank and the glow of a camp-fire appeared up ahead in the blackness, Gower tensed. This was very new to him, and he didn't know how he would react in the face of danger. From what he knew of the down-and-outs in New York, they refused to betray those of their own ilk, or anyone on the wrong side of the law.

'Eight of them,' O'Neill whispered, counting the number of tramps squatting round a fire as he and Gower moved closer.

Unaware of their presence, the hoboes drank coffee from castaway tin cans as they engaged in animated conversation. They went quiet as O'Neill and Gower stepped out of the shadows into the reddish light of the fire. Mistaking them for fellow hungry, homeless beings in need of the cosy warmth of the fire, the squatting tramps shuffled up to make room for O'Neill and Gower.

Remaining on his feet, O'Neill

stepped closer to the fire so that the hoboes could see that he wasn't one of them. Looking from one to the other of the half-shadowed faces, he said, 'There's been a lot of thieving from the railroad.'

The group remained silent. O'Neill jabbed a pointing finger at the oldest man there, who had a powerful-looking dog sitting at his side. With long, straggly white hair and a silky beard, the oldster looked frightened as O'Neill asked, 'What do you know about it?'

'Don't tell him nothing, Dad,' a tramp hunkering in the circle behind O'Neill called out.

O'Neill swiftly backhanded the tramp, the force of the blow sending him in a backward somersault. As O'Neill took a step nearer to the old man, the dog snarlingly bared its teeth.

'Down, Towser,' the old tramp commanded the dog, then addressed O'Neill. 'It ain't us doing the stealing, Bo.'

'But you know who it is.'

The old head shook, sending the white hair swinging wildly. 'Couldn't tell you, Bo.'

Moving fast O'Neill grasped the old man by his ragged shoulder and pulled him to his feet. A horrified Gower then saw O'Neill release the shoulder and slam the white-haired man heavily across the side of the head. Even though delivered with the open hand, it was a knock-down blow. As the old hobo was falling to the ground, his dog flew at O'Neill. The long yellow teeth of the animal seemed about to close on O'Neill's thigh, when the soldier brought up a knee sharply. O'Neill's knee hit the dog squarely under the jaw, noisily slamming its mouth closed and snapping its head back cruelly. Letting out a long whine of pain, the dog hurtled through the air and crashed to the ground. It lay with its head at a grotesque angle from the body, whimpering and convulsing pitifully.

Sickened by this, Gower expected the other tramps to jump on O'Neill, but they were all too frightened of him. He dragged the old tramp to his feet, holding him upright by gripping his tattered coat at the chest. Gower saw tears glisten in the white-haired hobo's eyes as he turned his gaze to where his distressed dog lay.

'Start talking, old man,' O'Neill ordered menacingly.

'Uniforms,' the tramp gasped. 'Men wearing soldiers' clothes.'

'Who leads them?'

When the white-haired man didn't reply, O'Neill drew back his free arm, fist clenched. The tramp shuddered in fear and lay the fingers of his left hand across the sleeve of his right upper arm. 'He has badges here.'

'Chevrons?'

The white head nodded vigorously. 'Chevrons, yes. Three chevrons.'

'Name?'

'I don't know his name, Bo.'

Shaking the oldster violently, O'Neill repeated his question. 'Name?'

'Dellinski.'

'Lee Dellinski,' a satisfied O'Neill said with a nod.

Suddenly released, the white-haired tramp collapsed on the ground, but he swiftly scrambled to his knees and crawled rapidly over to his dog, which now lay quietly. Something inside Gower withered as he saw the old man collapse across the body of the dog, sobbing uncontrollably.

Already walking away from the camp, O'Neill said, 'Come on, Gower, we could have a long night ahead of us.'

'There was no need to be so hard on that old man,' Gower protested, as he fell in beside O'Neill.

'I had a job to do, and that was the only way to do it,' O'Neill shrugged. 'You'd best go back to the hotel right now, Gower, as things are going to get a whole lot tougher when I catch up with Dellinski.'

Gower shook his head. 'I'm not going back. Do you know this Dellinski?'

'I know him. Lee Dellinski is the craziest, meanest creature out West,

Gower. He deserted at Bull Run,' O'Neill explained.

'Surely that means he's a coward.'

'All it means,' O'Neill said, with a short, harsh chuckle, 'is that Dellinski had to get away because he'd shot and killed a major on his own side.'

Though determined not to give O'Neill any satisfaction by backing out, the brutal treatment of the old hobo combined with having learned what sort of a man they were after led Gower to wish fervently that he was back in New York.

3

They had ridden all night and the rising sun was adding a sparkle to the pinnacles of the high ground up ahead when O'Neill pulled up and studied the ground carefully. Waiting for the army man to explain what was likely to happen, Gower was disappointed. Moving on to lead them into a deep canyon, all O'Neill said as he glanced up at the towering walls was, 'Once you start down this trail you can't get off even if you want to.'

It worried Gower that O'Neill reckoned on this being a lengthy expedition. He was expected at the end of the line where the track laying was said to be pushing ahead fast. That was where his work for the Union Pacific should begin; not here at North Platte chasing after a few inconsequential robbers with Liam O'Neill, a man whom for all his military discipline was untamed.

Further on, the lieutenant dismounted and hunkered to study a faint muddle of hoofprints. O'Neill commented, 'Seems like we bear off to the right. We use that passage instead of the main canyon.'

It was just a gap in the wall, a tortuous passage that took them round a series of sharp angles. O'Neill was constantly watching the ground, obviously certain that they were following a robbers' path. It was noon when a change came with such abruptness that it took Gower by surprise. Just beyond a bend in the passage, the rimrock ended and directly in front of them was a valley. It was a pleasant meadow set squarely in the heart of a wasteland.

To their left, stood a crude shack at the foot of a frowning precipice. A column of smoke trickled up from the shack into the noon sky. Four tethered horses grazed close to the shack, which could only be approached across flat land.

'Just four of them,' a pleased O'Neill remarked. He may have seen odds of four to two as reasonable, but Gower didn't share his view.

O'Neill, holding the reins with one hand, drew his rifle from its scabbard before going on, 'Put that rifle I gave you ready across the saddle in front of you, Gower.'

'What do you plan to do, O'Neill?'

With a short, snorting laugh, O'Neill replied, 'In this sort of situation, where there's no way you can creep up on them, a plan isn't possible. We just ride on up to that shack and leave it to them to make their move.'

'Which could be to shoot us out of the saddle,' a tense Gower pointed out.

'You've been sitting in New York reading those trashy books about the Wild West,' O'Neill chuckled. 'Most of the fellas out here, whether they are bad or good, couldn't hit a barn door from six feet.'

'What if those men in there are an

exception to that theory of yours?' Gower asked.

'Then a bullet in your head will stop you fretting about this new job of yours,' O'Neill grinned, his perception impressing Gower. Then he offered a strategy that provided Gower with some reassurance, albeit scant. 'We'll ride straight up to test them out. If they should start shooting we split. You ride for that little brook to the left, where you can take cover and pick off anyone making for the horses. I'll try to make it to that little clump of pines to the right.'

This meant that O'Neill would have a much greater distance to ride before gaining cover, and Gower didn't envy him. They kept their horses at walking pace as they advanced on the shack. Despite the four horses outside, Gower was convincing himself that the shack was unoccupied. But then a burst of action erupted with bewildering speed. As the door was yanked open and two men spilled out in a scrambling rush, a rifle spurted flame at the window and the slug passed between O'Neill and Gower, whistling as it went.

'Move, Gower!'

As O'Neill shouted, they both jabbed the spurs in hard. Their mounts leapt into an instant gallop, and Gower heard O'Neill's yelled instructions. 'Those two are going for the horses. Get to that brook and stop them.'

Though Gower moved fast, it wasn't good enough. The two men had freed their horses and were leaping up into the saddle before he had dismounted. Dropping to his knees behind the low bank of the brook, Gower brought his rifle up. Heading away from him, the backs of the two riders presented targets that were within range, but he hesitated. By the time he had curled his finger on the trigger it was too late.

Realizing that he had not wanted to shoot either of the men made Gower feel guilty. Someone was still firing from the window of the shack, which told him that O'Neill had made it to the pines, but the rifleman had him pinned down. O'Neill had been relying on him, and by allowing the two men to get away, Gower had let him down.

Raising his head above the bank, his presence making the two remaining tethered horses nervously restless, Gower noted that the firing from the shed had ceased. A slight movement caught his eye. At first he wasn't sure, but then he was certain that the door of the shack was slowly opening again. To his right, he saw O'Neill come out from behind a tree to stand with his shoulder against it, rifle raised in a firing position.

There were two men left to come out, and Gower told himself firmly that this time he would have to shoot. If he didn't, then it was likely that the robbers would get both O'Neill and him.

The door crashed open the final part of the way. It was just one man who sprung out into the open. O'Neill was fast, firing his rifle while Gower was still assessing the situation. The running man swerved, staggered, then fell to his knees, dropping the rifle he had been carrying in one hand. Gower's assumption that O'Neill had hit the man proved to be wrong. Coming up on to his feet fast, he came running at a crouch towards the horses and where Gower was concealed by the bank. Once again Gower hesitated, this time waiting for a second shot to come from O'Neill. But another rifle barked, and Gower could see that the fourth man was on the roof of the shack, his shot sending O'Neill back behind the pines.

'That's Dellinski, Gower,' O'Neill, forced to take cover, shouted. 'Get him!'

Rifle held at waist level, finger on the trigger, Gower stood up. Using the horses as a shield from O'Neill, the man was between them and Gower, just feet away. Bending to untie one of the horses, he became aware of Gower and stood to turn slowly to face him. He wore an army uniform, the dark blue of it faded, dusty and torn. All that remained of any former glory was the bright gold of the sergeant's chevrons on each sleeve. Having dropped his rifle and with no chance to draw the gun holstered at his hip, Dellinski spread his hands apart in a gesture of half surrender.

Gower found himself looking into the hardest face he had ever seen. It was a collection of sharp angles. The dark skin made it seem that the features had been roughly carved out of mahogany. Everything about it was disproportionate; the nose too thick, the mouth too wide, and the jaw-line too pronounced. Two small, black and exceedingly bright eyes were fixed on Gower, who knew what he had to do and was ordering himself to pull the trigger.

He might have been able to shoot had Dellinski shown fear, or if he had begged for his life. But Delliniski just stood there, coolly prepared to die, and he even gave a long-toothed smile as if to encourage Gower to pull the trigger and get it over with. O'Neill had said that Dellinski was crazy, and it was now clear to Gower that he was facing a madman. It was so unnerving that Gower's trigger-finger froze. O'Neill was shouting something but Gower couldn't hear what it was. The rifleman up on the roof was continuing to fire at fairly regular intervals.

Suddenly, Dellinski laughed. It was a brief but genuinely amused burst of laughter that made the face harder, even uglier. Then he confidently turned his back on Gower and walked to a horse. Watching the man go, Gower knew that he had to stop him; to fire the rifle, but he just couldn't bring himself to do it. Dellinski swung up into the saddle and, as he moved the horse away, an exasperated O'Neill took a chance by coming out round the tree and firing a shot at him. It was a hasty shot, and it went wide. O'Neill was deprived of another shot by a volley from the man on the shed roof.

Aware of O'Neill yelling at him,

Gower stood as still as a statue as he watched Dellinski ride away. It was the feel of something plucking at his trouser leg and burning his thigh that brought him back to life. Realizing that the man on top of the shed had fired at him, Gower reacted instinctively. Doing a fast quarter-turn, he fired the rifle from his hip. He saw the man stand up, appear to stretch himself, arms above his head, until he took a couple of steps backward before pitching forwards and sliding from the roof.

O'Neill was there when the rifleman plunged to the ground with a thud. Using a foot to turn him on to his back, the soldier looked up as Gower approached. 'Dead,' he announced. 'That was a good shot.' Not answering, Gower experienced an inner trembling. This was the first time that he had ever taken a life, and he found that he was unable to look down at the man he had killed.

'First blood,' O'Neill said, gesturing with his head to the dead man. 'You've crossed the border into the killing lands, Gower. It'll come easier to you from now on.'

Gower silently dismissed what O'Neill had said. His regret over killing one man was so painful that he was convinced he would never kill again. He said humbly, 'I'm sorry that I let Dellinski get away.'

'You will be sorry, I guess,' O'Neill predicted ominously. 'Did that crazy man get a look at you?'

'We were face to face,' Gower replied with an inward shiver as he recalled the way Dellinski's black-eyed gaze had probed deeply into him.

'Then he'll have marked you down, Gower.'

'Why?'

'Because you could have killed him, should have killed him, but didn't,' O'Neill answered. 'By not pulling the trigger of your rifle you will have insulted Lee Dellinski.'

That was preposterous, Gower told himself. He had spared Dellinski's life, for which he would surely be grateful. He complained to O'Neill, 'That doesn't make sense.'

'Nothing about Lee Dellinski makes sense,' O'Neill said cryptically. 'Come on, let's take a look-see in the shack.'

Inside the shack they could see supplies of all kinds, including ammunition, stacked to the roughhewn ceiling. With a pleased grin, O'Neill predicted, 'I guess Glendon will be mighty pleased to send wagons out to take this lot back.'

Glendon was more than pleased when they returned to North Platte. He was delighted, and heaped praise on both Gower and O'Neill for their good work in recovering the stolen property. He promptly organized wagons to go out to retrieve the stolen supplies, then came smilingly back to Gower and O'Neill.

'I'll send word explaining why you'll be late reaching the end of track,' Glendon promised. 'Tonight I want you both at my daughter's birthday ball here in the hotel. That way I'll be able to thank you both properly.'

Fully expecting O'Neill to complain that Dellinski and two of his men had escaped, and report his ineffectiveness, Gower was astonished and relieved when the lieutenant said nothing. As a city man, the thought of attending a social event that evening thrilled him, particularly after his first experience of roughing it in the wilds. He was also surprised, and more than a little ashamed, of the effect that the thought of meeting Mercedes Glendon again had on him.

At the ball that evening it affected Gower even more to discover that Mercedes sought his company. Though realizing that this was largely due to her preference for the sophistication of a New York man to the less civilized manner of the majority of the males present, he knew that wasn't the full answer. Liam O'Neill, perfectly groomed and smartly uniformed, was every inch an officer and a gentleman in these surroundings, but Mercedes wasn't affording him anything like the attention she was Gower.

'You are an expert dancer, sir,' she complimented Gower, as they moved gracefully in a waltz. 'You fair put me to shame.'

'Probably the sign of a dissipated life,' he joked to avoid saying that dancing had been the favourite pursuit of his wife and himself. This was the first time he'd held another woman in his arms since meeting Lola, and it was an experience that stirred conflicting emotions in him.

Mercedes smiled up at him. She wore an elegant ball-gown that Gower guessed was a Paris import costing anything up to a $1,000. Her hair was parted in the middle and pulled smooth over her temples, with ringlets over her ears.

'I would never believe that for a moment.' Suddenly indecisive, she paused. Then she said, 'My father told me about your appointment to the

Union Pacific. I find it so difficult to understand why a man like yourself would want to forsake city life for the kind of environment to which you are headed.'

'My reasons for leaving New York were both personal and compelling . . . ' Gower began, but an embarrassed Mercedes interrupted.

'Forgive me. I have this awfully rude kind of curiosity. I've offended you, and I am sorry.'

'You have no need to apologize, Miss Glendon. If I sounded somewhat abrupt, it was unintentional,' he said quickly. 'It is a matter of unhappy memories.'

'Then I am sorry that I have made you sad.'

'I have no intention of spoiling your birthday with my self-pity,' he smiled at her. 'My hope is that you might favour me with another dance before the evening ends?'

'Now let me see,' a blushing Mercedes mused, before adding archly, 'selfishly, I have not promised anyone a dance, hoping that you would be with me all evening.'

Staggered by this, Gower enquired, 'The last waltz?'

'Especially the last waltz,' Mercedes answered, her face now crimson. 'It worries me that your work will be extremely dangerous. It will be necessary to ride out into what is a wilderness. There will be hostile Indians and bands of desperate men as well.'

'I'll have Lieutenant O'Neill and his troop to protect me.'

Gower felt a stab of jealousy as she looked intently across the room at Liam O'Neill. He was talking to a well-dressed older man. Gower noticed that O'Neill, though never a man to become animated, appeared to be annoyed or angry and was arguing with the middle-aged man.

A pensive Mercedes spoke so quietly that she seemed to be talking to herself rather than Gower. 'Lieutenant O'Neill is a danger in himself.'

There was something happening at the end of the room. A lot of people seemed to be moving about there, but Gower couldn't get a clear view because of the other dancers. The music stopped, the dance ended and the man O'Neill had been in conversation with climbed up on the rostrum to stand beside the three fiddlers who had been making the music.

At Gower's side, Mercedes leaned close to whisper, 'That's Thomas Durant, the vice-president and general manager of the Union Pacific Railroad.'

Durant wasn't what Gower expected a man in his position to be. His hair was a little thin on top and greying at the temples. He was heavily lined, but that was due to living an outdoor life rather than ageing. The lines were sharp, and his dark complexion was that of a permanent tan that lasts all year round.

'Don't worry, folks,' Durant addressed the assembly. 'I am not going to bore you with a long speech. This night belongs to the lovely Mercedes, and you'll join me in wishing her a happy birthday.'

The crowd and Durant intoned in unison: 'Happy birthday, Mercedes.' As all heads turned her way, she was blushing an even deeper red than before.

Recommencing his speech, Durant said, 'I know that all of you are as interested in the progress of the railroad as I am.' He paused until the shouts of assent had died down. 'Depending on the availability of materials, we have been moving west at one to three miles a day.' Again he paused, this time to allow applause to fade away. 'Now hear this, my dear friends. It has been reported to me that recently eight and one-half-miles of track were laid in a single day.'

This was greeted with clapping and wild cheering, which had a smiling Durant preen himself up on the rostrum. As the ovation ended, so did a quiet voice at Gower's left side bitterly ask a question without expecting an answer. 'How many extra dead per mile did that mean?'

Turning his head, Gower found Liam O'Neill standing beside him. The lieutenant was not his usual laconic self. Gower said, 'I don't understand, O'Neill.'

'You will understand, very soon, Gower. They brag now and they'll be boasting forever when the railroad is finished. One thing they'll never tell us is how many lives it cost per mile.'

'Surely it's not that bad?' an incredulous Gower enquired, baffled by O'Neill's change of loyalties. Something had upset him that evening, and Gower wondered if it was the attention that Mercedes was paying him.

'It's worse,' O'Neill said. 'A man's life isn't worth a bent nickel to Thomas Durant, and that includes your life, Gower.'

'I've been hired to do a job, O'Neill, and I'll do it.'

'Do or die, and you'll most likely die,'

O'Neill remarked cynically. 'Take a train back to New York in the morning, Gower. That's my advice.'

'I don't need your advice, O'Neill.'

'If you're lucky you might live long enough to regret not taking it,' O'Neill said as he walked away.

4

The scenery on the final leg of his journey had fascinated Gower. He had marvelled at how the Union Pacific had bridged ravines with trestles and the way ridges had been carved and blasted through. Now, in an alien but exciting world west of Cheyenne, he learned from a proud Thomas Durant how progress had been made despite a chronic labour shortage caused by most able-bodied men preferring to try and strike it rich in the gold in mines.

'We were lucky though,' Durant went on, as they stood together watching tracks being laid. Behind them were twenty carriages in which the crews lived. These included dormitories and an arsenal car containing a thousand loaded rifles. 'We managed to recruit more than ten thousand Chinamen who were originally aiming for the gold fields.'

The sheer scale of the track-laying and the smoothness of the operation both amazed and impressed Gower. Just two men were in charge, and one of them, a huge, rough-looking fellow incongruously dressed as a Cossack, had total command of the large crew.

Durant identified the two men for Gower. 'That's the Casement brothers, Dan and Jack. The guy in the Cossack outfit is Jack. He doubles as the top hand and the law out here. If anyone cuts up rough, then Jack sees to it. We've some tough characters out here, Gerald. Some of our Irish workers put the wind up me just to look at them, but nobody's yet got the better of Jack, and I don't reckon as how anyone ever will.'

'Looking at him, I can believe that,' Gower said, as Jack Casement bellowed an order and dozens of men obeyed him instantly.

The track-laying was a science that

absorbed Gower. Though the men worked knee-deep in alkali dust, the teamwork was carried out with admirable precision. A single horse drawing a light car galloped up to the front with a load of steel rails taken from a flatbed railway freight car that was halted a few yards back along the line. Two men stepped up to seize the end of a rail and move forward, with the rest of the gang taking hold by twos until the rail was clear of the car. Then they ran with the rail and, at the shouted command of 'Down' from Jack Casement they dropped the rail in its place. This last move was carried out carefully so that the rail was positioned right side up. At the same time, on the other side of the freight car, the process was duplicated. Gower timed the operation. Each rail took less than thirty seconds to lay, which meant that four rails went down to the minute.

No time was wasted when the freight car was empty. The gang tipped it bodily over on the side of the track to let the next loaded car pass by. Then the empty car was righted on the track and pulled away for another load by a galloping horse on the end of sixty to eighty feet of rope. Close behind the track-layers came the gaugers, spikers and bolters, moving with speed and rhythm. The ring of sledge-hammers against iron had a steady beat that was almost tuneful.

'The Anvil Chorus,' an amused Durant commented on the sound.

'This is something that has to be seen to be believed,' an awed Gower said.

'I can imagine what seeing this for the first time must be like,' Durant assented with a nod. 'But this is just one part of a whole, Gerald, and the role you have to play makes you as an individual more important than all those labourers put together.

'There's anything from one hundred up to two hundred farmers up ahead. They aren't going to take kindly to moving out, Gerald, but they all have to go. The Union Pacific can't allow sentiment to stand in the way of progress. But we want the farmers moved out peaceable. The Union Pacific has the backing of Congress now, but that could be put at risk by any adverse publicity. Everything depends not only on your legal skill but also your diplomacy.'

'I understand that, sir, and I will do my very best.'

'I know that you will, Gerald,' Durant said, slapping him on the shoulder. 'You will be leaving here with Lieutenant O'Neill in the morning. We have worked the schedule out carefully. You have a long ride to the farms, Gerald. But by the time you get there and carry out your legal work, we will be approaching with the track. The railroad's timing has to be precise at all times. We can't afford the slightest delay, which is what makes your work so important.'

Not having realized this was how it would be, Gower was relieved that he would be making only a one-way ride through hostile territory. Even so, he found it daunting to contemplate that ride and the dangers it would entail. The responsibility that negotiating with the farmers placed upon him was worrying.

'I'll need to know what scope I have in dealing with the farmers, sir.'

'It's all been put down on paper and is waiting for you in my office, Gerald,' Durant assured him. 'Now, I must go as I have several meetings to attend.'

Gower regretted that Durant was about to leave him. He found that he liked the railroad chief. Maybe he was given to the occasional boast, but Gower could see nothing about Durant that merited O'Neill's intense dislike that appeared to amount to hatred.

O'Neill walked up in his relaxed manner soon after Durant had gone. Out of uniform, wearing buckskin, again, he showed his customary supercilious attitude towards Gower. Taking a disinterested look at the brute human effort of the track laying, he asked, 'Did

Durant tell you?'

'Only that we are leaving in the morning. Nothing more than that.'

'That's Durant for you, careful to leave out the bad bit,' O'Neill said with short, harsh laugh. 'Ten men is all they can spare me.'

Having anticipated a troop of some forty or fifty soldiers, Gower asked, 'Why's that?'

'There are constant Indian attacks here in the field. They strike without warning and have run off railroad stock by the thousand,' O'Neill explained. 'Numbers of workers have been killed, so Durant wants most of my men and my sergeant to stay here to protect Union Pacific interests and personnel.'

'Can't you get more troopers sent in?' Gower enquired.

The lieutenant shook his head. 'No. The Union Pacific is supposed to have its own private army. My men and me are here unofficially, through some arrangement between General Sherman, commander of the military

71

division of the West and Grenville Dodge, the Union Pacific chief engineer. Dodge was a Union general in the war.'

Logic suddenly eased Gower's worry about riding out with so few troopers. Thomas Durant had told him that there were up to 200 families farming land up ahead. If they were safe from the Indians, then surely O'Neill and he would be equally secure. He put this theory to O'Neill, getting a mirthless smile in return.

'The farmers are a long way from here, Gower, and we have to pass through territory occupied by the Sioux to get to them. Apart from an occasional raid by wild young bucks, the Indians don't bother the farmers because the farmers don't bother them. It's the railroad that the Sioux see as the enemy, with good reason.'

'Why are the Indians against the railroad?' Gower asked, guessing that it was a silly question, and ashamed of his ignorance.

O'Neill didn't mock him, but explained. 'Bison are the source of food, clothing and shelter for the plains tribes. The railroad is splitting up the great herds of bison, and will be bringing out hunters to kill them off. Naturally, the Sioux want to protect their families and homeland.'

'I suppose ten soldiers are better than none at all.' Gower tentatively gave his opinion as he pondered on what O'Neill had told him.

'I wouldn't be too sure of that,' O'Neill said. 'The sight of just eleven bluecoats will have the Sioux attack, bringing us trouble we won't be able to handle.'

Shaken by this, Gower asked, 'Are you saying that so few troopers will increase the risk we'll be taking?'

'That's exactly what I'm saying,' O'Neill nodded. 'I still think you should take the next train back to New York, Gower.'

'I think not,' Gower said, though his resolve was secretly wavering.

His misgivings about the venture had increased tenfold by the time night fell. Gower slept a fitful sleep that was disturbed by ominous dreams. In the morning, as he saw O'Neill heading his way, he found himself hoping that the bad dreams hadn't been premonitions.

O'Neill turned out in uniform, smart enough to be going on an official parade. The lieutenant's handsome face wore a steely expression, a reminder for Gower of the tough time that was ahead of them. Checking that Gower still had the rifle, O'Neill passed him a heavy six-shooter, saying, 'Shove that in the waistband of your pants, Gower. You don't need a gunbelt and holster where we're going. There'll be no call for a fast draw.'

The camp was stirring behind them. For Gower there was a strange feeling of security in seeing the pick and shovel men, the teamsters, blacksmiths, masons, carpenters, mechanics and track layers prepare to begin another day of labour. It was a security that he was reluctant to leave.

The shrilling of a bugle brought about an irregular stampede of soldiers from their tents. They quickly formed up in regular ranks for the day's muster parade. Orders were shouted, the voices of command ringing clearly on the morning air. A party of ten troopers fell out to mount horses and line up behind O'Neill who was astride a big black stallion. Though he found it impossible to like the coldly aloof lieutenant, Gower had to concede that O'Neill made an imposing figure when he took on his military duties.

As the lieutenant led his small group out of camp in single file, Gower mounted up to ride beside him. Looking out over the sage-green desert shimmering under a rising sun was an experience that Gower's nervousness spoiled for him. The crags of the lofty mountains far up ahead were brilliant saw teeth in the sunrise. It was still early enough for Gower to shiver a little in the wind that spilled down from the faraway peaks.

O'Neill and the big black stallion he rode obviously had a lot in common. A bond of affection between them was easy to detect. The lieutenant's wide shoulders and lean flanks harmonized well with the sturdy body and clean limbs of the horse. There was an understanding between the man and the animal that was beyond the senses. They knew each other well.

O'Neill had set a slow pace that wouldn't tire the horses. They had ridden for an hour without speaking, when they rounded a rocky bend to come face to face with three Indians mounted on scraggy ponies. Raising a hand to halt his party, O'Neill quietly instructed Gower, 'Don't make any sudden moves, Gower, and keep your hands away from that rifle.'

At first Gower was puzzled as to why the experienced O'Neill had ridden straight into what looked to be a serious situation. But then Gower realized that something about the lieutenant's attitude as they had neared the bend had suggested that he knew someone was approaching.

The three red men reined up facing them. The centre Indian eased his mount a little forward. Gower assumed that this was to distinguish himself as the leader. The Indian was thin, agile, and wary. His braided hair was a jet black, as were his sombre eyes. When O'Neill raised one hand in friendly greeting, the Indian's coppery countenance didn't change, but he watched a little more keenly.

Keeping a strict vigil, O'Neill spoke out the side of his mouth to Gower. 'This is Grey Elk. He has no English and I can't handle the Indian language. Grey Elk has never given any trouble, but you can never be certain of the vagaries of a full-blood Sioux. Something simple can send them mad enough to throw a tomahawk or fire a gun.'

Accepting that O'Neill wanted him to stay quiet and still in the saddle,

Gower gladly obeyed. This was his first encounter with so-called savages, and the three redskins were too close for his liking. He watched O'Neill and Grey Elk sign-talk. Both men grunted and pointed a lot. Gower was learning fast and was able to read some of the signs. Black Elk spread his hands with palms up, which Gower took to mean day, and then put one hand on top of the other for night. Then his hands that were the shade of a leather boot were clenching and unclenching fast the fingers flying out straight each time.

Counting, Gower tallied one hundred, and was aware of a frown of concern creasing O'Neill's handsome and normally expressionless face. The lieutenant made more signs that Gower deciphered as a question, a request for confirmation. Grey Elk responded by again making the one day and one night signs with his hands.

With a satisfied nod, O'Neill made a gesture by passing a hand and arm across his chest. When the Indian copied the gesture, Gower came to the conclusion that it meant the talk was over and both sides should go in peace.

Turning in his saddle, O'Neill called an order back to his men. The soldiers moved their mounts sideways to permit the three Indians to ride on past. The Sioux went without looking either to the left or right. Then the troopers regained their former position, and when O'Neill gave a 'forward' signal with his right hand, they moved off behind him at the same slow pace as before. Then O'Neill gave a second signal and they were moving so fast that Gower had to spur his horse to catch up with the lieutenant. Whatever had been conveyed by the Indian to the lieutenant had obviously caused a change in plan.

'What's happening, O'Neill?'

'There's at least a hundred redskins, the largest raiding party yet, riding in to attack the construction camp. They are just a day and a night away from us now.'

The vast size of the territory had Gower ask a question he already had the answer to. 'We can avoid them, let them go on by?'

'We could, easily, but we can't do that.'

'We have to, O'Neill,' Gower insisted. 'Our task is to get to those farms as soon as we can.'

'I won't argue on that score, Gower, but my *duty* as an army officer is to protect those people back at the camp.'

Alarmed by what O'Neill was implying, Gower said, 'We can't go back.'

'I know that,' O'Neill said, shaking his head at what he saw as Gower's stupidity. 'What we can do is make sure the redskins don't make it to the construction camp.'

Realization dawned on Gower, chilling him. They were riding fast to engage the Sioux raiding party. Fighting to keep his voice steady, he argued, 'There's a hundred or more of them, O'Neill. You have just ten men.'

'It's all a matter of strategy, Gower.

Strategy and tactics,' O'Neill said, 'which is something I know all about but of which those hostiles heading our way are ignorant.'

Gower decided that O'Neill was either foolishly reckless or deranged. It was probably the latter. Although he was not a fighting man, common sense told Gower that there was nothing that would enable ten men to take on one hundred and survive.

Halting his troop in the shallow gulch of a dry river between tall, shouldering buttes and bluffs, O'Neill rode halfway down the file. Arrowheads of geese shot over their heads as he reined up, addressing his men from the saddle. 'There's a Sioux war party coming our way. It's heading for the construction camp, and we are going to intercept it at the Singing Hills Lake. That means we need to keep riding all night so that we can cross the Dark Bear River in the early dawn hours.

That night passed more quickly than Gower had thought possible. At first light with wedges of wild ducks flying overland and alighting on an open stream, they rode through fringing willows and dogwoods butted round the water edges, to cross the river.

Heading towards distant green hilltops, they traversed an open space so vast that Gower's mind had difficulty accepting it. He found the contrast to the streets of New York flanked by high buildings, to be disorienting. With a perfumed wind caressing the land with Chinook hands softer than those of any woman, it was so peaceful that Gower came close to forgetting that they were riding towards a gun battle.

But he remembered clearly at noon when they stopped to water horses and stretch their saddle-cramped limbs. O'Neill was studying a near cloudless sky when Gower asked, 'When will we get to this lake?'

'I want to be there at sundown,' O'Neill replied. 'Grey Elk says a young chief, a half-blood named Johnny Starr, is leading the party. I know Johnny well enough to be sure just where he'll camp at the lake. We'll skirt round to move in from the west with the setting sun behind us. They won't see us until we start firing.'

'There's a whole lot of Indians to fire at,' an unconvinced Gower reminded the lieutenant.

'My men will make every bullet count. Leave the fighting to me, Gower,' O'Neill advised, adding an order, 'but make sure that you use that rifle this time.'

'I'll use it,' Gower promised.

But his confidence had faded when at twilight they were moving stealthily on foot, spread out over smoothly rolling banks and through ancient lake beaches laced with flourishing groves of birch. Rifle held in both hands across his chest, Gower froze in mid-step at a frantic signal from O'Neill who was over to his right. Bewildered for a moment, Gower then saw the shadowy figure of an Indian close in front of him, sitting on the ground with his back against a tree. The Sioux was no more than a boy. Obviously having been posted as a lookout, he was unaware of Gower's presence. He was smiling in amusement at an insect that was running in different directions over a raised hand that he twisted this way and that.

Some eight feet away, O'Neill drew a long-bladed knife from a sheath and drew the dull edge of it lightly across his own throat. Gower got the message: O'Neill wanted him to slit the young Indian's throat. It made him thankful that he didn't carry a knife. He signalled back to O'Neill that he had no knife.

Gower's heart sank as O'Neill made signs that he would throw his knife to him. With urgent hand movements, O'Neill impressed on Gower that he must catch the knife. To drop it would alert the Indian.

The knife came at him fast. Gower plucked it out of the air, luckily by the handle. Filled with dread, Gower turned his attention back to the young Indian. If the whole Sioux camp wasn't to be alerted, which would mean the deaths of O'Neill, himself, and every soldier there, he had to kill the Indian boy, swiftly and noiselessly.

Even as he clutched the knife and brought his arm up ready, Gerald Gower knew that he couldn't do it. Reminding himself that there was no alternative, he dropped to a crouch. A sudden sound from the Indian startled him, his body going rigid. Then the sound came again. The Indian boy was laughing softly at the insect as the tiny creature scurried up and down his fingers.

That muted laughter brought the situation into horrific clarity. Sinking back on his heels, a suddenly exhausted Gower felt sweat break out all over his body to immediately go icy cold on his skin. He knew that the lives of O'Neill and his troopers depended on him right then. But he couldn't kill a human being. There was no way that he could slit the throat of or plunge a blade deep into a young boy who was still chuckling delightedly to himself.

5

Sweat ran stingingly into Gower's eyes. Raising the hand holding the knife, he wiped his sleeve across his forehead to clear his vision. Then a hand gripped his wrist and took the knife. O'Neill was standing close to him, the knife in one of his hands and the forefinger on his other hand to his lips to caution silence. How the lieutenant had reached his side without making a sound astonished Gower.

Moving against the narrow tree trunk, O'Neill reached to clamp his left hand over the mouth of the Sioux boy. Then his right hand brought the knife round to slash the razor sharp blade across the smooth, brown-skinned throat.

A horrified Gower saw the small body of the Indian flopping around grotesquely in the undergrowth. Blood pumped from the gashed throat that had the look of an enormously wide and laughing red-lipped mouth. The rapid loss of blood caused the body to shrink so that it seemed no bigger than that of a baby when at last it ceased all movement.

Gower heard himself whispering prayers for the boy as a calm O'Neill signalled to his men to move forwards. Thickening trees made it darker as they moved closer. At the tip of the inky cone cast by the tree growth, Gower made out vague shapes on the ground that he took to be sleeping Sioux. Other Indians moved in the shadows, like sombre ghosts. To the left of the spectral figures he could detect the heads of ponies. Indian trained ponies, standing as motionless as mottled statues.

O'Neill was poised with his right arm raised above his head, waiting for his troopers to be in position before giving the order to open fire. The arm dropped swiftly and the night was torn apart by the reports of firing rifles. Capable of aiming at anonymous figures in the half-light, Gower pulled the trigger of his rifle again and again. Standing Indians reeled and fell. The inert bundles on the ground became animated, scrambling to their feet only to pitch forward on their faces as the merciless rifle fire ripped into the camp.

Though the Indians began to fight back, the red glare of a dying sun behind the soldiers meant that they were firing blind. The flashes from the muzzles of their rifles made them targets for the soldiers. Gower became aware of some Indians gliding away from the others to fade into the peripheral shadows of their camp. Fear of making a fool of himself stopped him from shouting to tell O'Neill what he had seen.

He regretted it within minutes when a trooper called a panicky warning to O'Neill, 'They're flanking us, sir.' Then the twilight was alive with the wild cries of the Sioux. The yelling came from the right and slightly to the rear. It was an eerie sound that was intended to unsettle the troopers, and it had an instant effect.

Becoming aware of the silhouettes of bewildered soldiers milling around, Gower was shattered as the noise from a fusillade of rifle fire accompanied the cries of the Indians. A bullet swished through the air close to Gower's head. Instinctively ducking, he could see troopers being mown down in a swathe of rifle fire. Sobbing between screams, a stricken man called out a woman's name over and over.

'Fall back! Fall back!' O'Neill yelled out an order. 'Fall back to the lake.'

The lieutenant's shout restored discipline to the military party. Three soldiers and Gower followed O'Neill, who was moving back through the trees, firing as he went. Gower gloomily assumed that the three were the only survivors out of ten troopers. The one closest to Gower tripped as he kept up a steady fire while walking backwards.

Though desperate to get away from the relentless Sioux rifles, Gower reached a hand down to the fallen man. His fingers sank into a warm, stickiness. Mystified, Gower bent to squint down through the poor light as bullets tore the bark from the tree above his head. He reeled back on realizing that the soldier hadn't tripped, and that he had dipped his fingers into the bloody morass that had been the lower part of the trooper's face.

Frantically wiping his hand on his trouser leg, Gower was knocked off balance as another soldier collided with him. Flat on his back, Gower was winded as the trooper came crashing down on top of him. Gower heard the death rattle in the soldier's throat. Pushing the body aside he scrambled to his feet and ran.

There came the thud of a pair of running feet behind him. The footsteps faltered. There was a grunt followed by the crashing of a body into the undergrowth. Gower reached the horses. The Indians had ceased firing and had stopped yelling. O'Neill was there holding one horse by the bridle and tossing the reins of another to Gower. The lieutenant said tersely, 'Mount up, fast. There's only you and me left, Gower.'

O'Neill shouted to him as he yanked the head of his black stallion round and dug in the spurs. 'They've gone for their horses. There aren't many Sioux left, but they'll be on our trail within minutes.'

Sensing the urgency, the horses clamped the bits between strong teeth as they charged along the edge of the lake. As they headed for the distant hills, Gower heard distant hoofbeats that told him the Sioux were in pursuit.

Passing through a short canyon, they moved up into a rugged sweep of towering rocks and sand hills, where O'Neill suddenly reined in and dismounted. Changing swiftly into his buckskins, he rolled a slicker round his uniform and tied it behind his saddle.

Pulling his rifle from its saddle scabbard, he told Gower, 'Get off your horse and bring your rifle.'

Gower followed O'Neill through a thicket that smelled of new leaves and an odour of sap. Moving into some cottonwoods, they stood in darkness looking down into the lighter shade of the canyon.

'There should be three of them, four at the most,' O'Neill predicted.

It had seemed to be around twenty Sioux shooting at them through the trees, which made O'Neill's estimate sound like wishful thinking. Though he hesitated to contradict O'Neill, Gower disagreed. 'I'd say there were more than three or four.'

'There are,' O'Neill conceded. 'I'd say we left twelve to fifteen alive but they'll have split up into small groups. They'll have fresh horses and work in relays so as to track us down no matter how long it takes.'

'So we could never out-run them.'

'Never. We killed a lot of Sioux back

there, and put a stop to any raid on the construction camp. They'll want revenge. We'd have got them all if I'd had enough men to cover our flanks.'

Three riders entered the canyon at the far end. They were pushing their ponies hard, intent only on catching up with their quarry.

'You take the one on our left, Gower,' O'Neill instructed. 'Leave the other two to me.'

The Indians drew closer fast. Gower dreaded the moment when he would have to pull the trigger. This was different to the indiscriminate firing into the Sioux camp. In his sights was a man, a living creature whose life he was about to take. Beside him, O'Neill fired twice in swift succession. As he saw two Indians topple from their saddles, Gower pulled the trigger of his rifle as a reaction. He watched the Sioux he had aimed at raise both arms above his head, like a trick rider in a New York circus.

But this was no stunt. The Indian

went over the rear of his horse backward to crash to the ground. A strange exultation rose up in Gower. A sense of power that was almost divine in its intensity surged through him. Though ashamed of himself, he couldn't control the thrill that came from killing a man.

'Come on, Gower. The next party will be on our tails soon.'

The thrill died in Gower. There was nothing. He felt completely empty, as if some large part of himself expired at the same time as the Sioux warrior he had killed.

'How far do we go before the next group catch up with us?' he asked.

'That depends.'

'On what?'

Guiding his black stallion through a tangle of greasewood, O'Neill replied, 'On whether or not Johnny Starr survived back at the lake. If he did, he'll change the plan when he comes across those three bucks we've left dead back in the canyon.'

'How will we know?'

'If Johnny Starr is alive, then you'll know,' O'Neill said grimly.

They rode on in the black silence of the pre-dawn, and soon a rising sun was streaking light across the eastern sky. O'Neill watched the slopes carefully, trying to judge the next place for an ambush from the rise and fall of the ground. The cold of the night still shrouded a valley they entered in the grey light of breaking day. Climbing steadily through foothills, they were approaching cliffs that appeared to be a rampart prohibiting any further advance.

O'Neill knew the way, through a twisting little valley where a brook gushed out through the cliffs. They climbed steeply until the rock opened out into a wider chasm. Then the lieutenant sent his stallion slanting up a stony path that brought them to the ledges that topped the cliff.

It was a hard climb. When they made it, O'Neill swung from the saddle, his eyes sweeping the rolling hills below. He said, 'We'll pitch the horses here out of sight.' Then he pointed to a ledge to their left. 'Then take up positions on that ledge.'

'Are they heading our way?' Gower enquired.

'Four of them this time.'

'Looks as if Johnny Starr is dead,' Gower remarked.

O'Neill said quietly, 'You can't be sure about anything with that half-blood. Johnny once warned me that he was more than my match in every way.'

'What's your opinion on that, O'Neill?'

'It's something that I hope never has to be proved,' O'Neill admitted.

The ledge was about twelve feet wide, with a low rocky cliff behind it. There was a clear view of the rocky path below that they had climbed.

'It won't be so easy this time,' O'Neill cautioned. 'Those four Sioux bucks will be expecting another ambush. We have only one way down, and those redmen could keep us pinned down up here forever.'

A worried Gower didn't comment. A suddenly conversational O'Neill said, 'I reckon you'll be real glad to get back to something that at least resembles civilization, Gower?'

'Only New York means civilization to me.'

This made O'Neill chuckle. 'It will be a long time before you see New York again. The way I see it you're going to have to settle for Askaro Bend for some time.'

'I've never heard of the place, O'Neill,' Gower said, tensing for a moment as his eye caught movement below. It was a bird that came wheeling back above some rocks.

'You'll soon get to know Askaro,' O'Neill assured him. 'It's not much of a town, but it stands at the end of the farming valley. They've fixed up a courtroom there for you to fight the legal claims some of the farmers are sure to make.'

'Wherever the courtroom is, I'll be more at home there than I am out here,' Gower responded.

'Mercedes Glendon will make you feel at home,' O'Neill said with a tight-lipped smile.

'I don't follow you, O'Neill.'

'Mercedes is the driving force behind her old man, and Samuel Glendon knows it. He's put her in charge of getting the land the government says the railway can have.'

Though he wouldn't welcome having a female boss, Mercedes was a special kind of woman, so having her in charge might compensate him for the time O'Neill predicted he would have to spend in Askaro Bend.

O'Neill exclaimed! 'Here they come!'

The four Indians rode their ponies in a different way to the previous three, more wary and alert. From their position on high he and O'Neill had the advantage, but it was an advantage that could be easily lost.

'We have to let them get real close,'

O'Neill advised, 'otherwise we might only get one or two, and spook the others.'

They turned their heads at the sound of gravel trickling behind them. A small stone rolled down in the wake of the gravel. There was no further warning. Three Indians leapt agilely down to land surefootedly on the narrow ledge. All three carried tomahawks, and Gower saw one strike O'Neill across the head, and then he was fully occupied as the other two Sioux came at him.

He brought his rifle up quickly. The first Indian was so close that the muzzle hit him in the mouth. The front sight caught under the Sioux's top lip, ripping it away, taking a section of nose and right cheek with it.

As the brave used both hands in an attempt at holding his torn, bleeding face together, Gower reversed his rifle to drive the butt deep into the Indian's midriff. In pain, the Sioux staggered close to the edge, and Gower nudged him over the edge with a knee. The

Sioux released a blood-chilling scream of terror as he hurtled down to the rocks below, while at the same time the second Indian jumped on Gower.

Smashed flat on his back with his head out over the drop, Gower was straddled by the Indian. The Sioux smelled, and even though the tomahawk was being raised to deliver what would be a fatal blow, Gower probed his memory to identify it. Then he remembered overhearing a man at the hotel in North Platte saying that the Indians rubbed bear fat on themselves.

The savage's tomahawk arm was swinging down. Working on instructions that came from some mysterious place deep inside him, Gower bucked his hips up off the ground. The timing was right. Catching the Sioux on the downward swing, the tomahawk just inches from Gower, it took him off balance. Going over Gower's head, the wide-eyed Indian tried to clutch at the ledge, but his fingers couldn't find a grip and he went silently plummeting down into the depths.

Sitting up, Gower saw O'Neill and the third Indian standing facing each other menacingly. Blood trickled down from O'Neill's skull, but he seemed unaffected by it. The Sioux was swarthy, his angular face like a mask. It struck Gower as ludicrous to see him pulling off a heavy plaid mackinaw as if he and O'Neill were having an argument in a bar room. Underneath he had on a flaming red flannel shirt.

Coming up on to one knee, Gower retrieved his rifle. The Indian's blood-shot eyes twitched warily in his direction, and though O'Neill had his back to Gower he seemed to know what was going on.

'Stay out of it,' O'Neill said hoarsely. 'This is strictly between me and Johnny Starr.'

So this was the half-blood whom O'Neill had hinted was his arch enemy. Gower was no expert, but he would never have guessed that Starr was only half Indian. He watched the crouching

O'Neill, every inch a fighter, draw the knife he had used to kill the Indian boy. Moving with a blurring speed, Starr kicked the knife out of O'Neill's hand and grabbed his arms.

Falling backwards in a planned move, his right foot in O'Neill's stomach, the half-blood threw the lieutenant over his head. Hitting the cliff wall hard, O'Neill slid down on to the ledge in an inert heap. On him in a flash, Starr drew his own knife. Straddling the helpless O'Neill, he grabbed his hair to pull his head back to expose his throat.

'No, Gower!' O'Neill croaked what could well be his last words as Gower stood with his rifle at the ready.

Gripping the wrist of Starr's knife hand, O'Neill applied what had to be superhuman strength to force the knife away from him. Dark veins stood out on the half-blood's forehead as he strained in an attempt at regaining control. But his muscle-packed body couldn't equal O'Neill's power. Slowly his arm gave way and he was at such a disadvantage that he tried to scramble off O'Neill so as to be in a position to change tactics.

O'Neill, though still holding Starr's wrist, appeared to be letting him move away. But then he gave a quick tug on the arm and the half-Sioux landed face down. He was about to roll away when O'Neill made a fast move. With both knees digging into Starr's back, O'Neill cupped his hands under the bony chin and pulled, putting the weight of his body behind it.

Face purpling, the half-blood's lips peeled back to bare gritted teeth. Then he began to foam at the mouth as O'Neill continued his relentless pressure. There was a crack as loud as a rifle being fired close at hand. Gower saw O'Neill quickly release Starr to avoid the thick dark blood that erupted from his mouth. At first believing that the half-blood's neck had snapped, Gower revised this theory when he remembered how loud the crack had been. It had to be Starr's spine that had broken.

On his feet now, O'Neill went cautiously to the edge to look down. Gower went with him to see that the worst had happened. The four Indians down below had dismounted and were carrying their rifles as they sought cover in the rocks. Gower despaired because he and O'Neill were now trapped on the ledge.

But O'Neill didn't seem to be worried. Going to Johnny Starr's body, he dragged it closer to the edge. Bending, he grasped a leg and an arm. Displaying unbelievable strength, he lifted the half-blood's body up above his head. With elbows locked, he walked to the rim. Letting out a howling yell that startled Gower, O'Neill threw the half-blood's body down.

Watching the explosion as flesh and bone disintegrated on the sharp rocks far below, Gower realized what O'Neill had planned to happen. The four Sioux rushed from cover to leap up on their ponies and gallop back the way they had come.

A cool O'Neill watched them go, saying to Gower, 'That's the last we'll see of them.' He smiled then. 'Come on, Gower, it's time to call on those farmers of yours.'

6

'I ain't got no fight left in me, son,' the old farmer said, 'so I guess whatever you and your railway wants to do to me and my place, I ain't about to stop you.'

Bent from years of toil, he wiped tears away with a khaki handkerchief. Wanting to believe that the tired old eyes were defective, Gower fervently hoped that the oldster wasn't crying. His wife, a weary, withered old woman, was huddled in a rickety chair. It was certain that she was weeping. A silent O'Neill stood by the window of the adobe building. It looked as if he was fascinated by something outside, but Gower knew that wasn't so. It had surprised Gower to find that the tough lieutenant was more distressed by serving notice on the farmers than he was.

'When the railroad moves into this

valley you stand to profit,' Gower offered the ageing couple what he hoped was some comfort.

The farmer's pale-grey eyes had distance in them. They were strange eyes that had a disturbing effect on Gower. Then the oldster broke the eye contact and pointed out of the window past O'Neill's head.

'Profit? What profit is there in losing the land you have worked, the land you love? There's no money that could pay for what we have put into this place, son, what it means to us.'

'I can understand that,' Gower said.

The head of sparse grey hair shook, and the old man's smile trembled. 'I don't think you can. You are too young. One day you will understand, but then it will be too late for me, and too late also for you.'

Those few simple words reached deep into Gower, causing him pain. For the first time since he had become a lawyer, Gerald Gower fully realized how profoundly people were affected by the work that he did. What to him were mere words and figures written on paper, meant happiness or misery, even life or death, to others. He forced himself to be professional, telling himself that he and what he had to offer was the best deal the farming folk in this valley were likely to get. The Union Pacific had government approval to simply seize the farms without paying compensation. Though they couldn't recognize the fact, he was the farmers' only hope. If he were to fail, then the Union Pacific could not spare the time to do anything other than ride rough-shod through the farming community.

Ill-at-ease, he gave the old man a curt nod and went out through the door. O'Neill followed closely on his heels. When they were mounted up, the old man came out. He stood frail and trembling, his lips silently forming words until at last he found his voice.

'How long?'

'Soon,' was all Gower could answer.

Their slow ride toward the next farm

gave Gower and O'Neill the chance to collect their thoughts. Gower still hadn't come to terms with having killed three Indians. His biggest difficulty was in accepting that the taking of life didn't mean as much to him as he would have expected. Since that time he found himself continually praying that he would never have to kill another man. But where O'Neill was concerned, the fight with the Sioux on the ledge had brought about a mutual respect that had improved their relationship, but now the business with the farmers was creating a new division between them. When they had ridden some distance without speaking, O'Neill broke the silence with a question.

'What will you do when your work here is finished, Gower, go back to New York?'

That was a possibility that had become more appealing to Gower of late. A post in the New York office of the Union Pacific Railway would suit him fine. His hope was that by the time this job out West was done he would have adjusted to Lola's death enough to settle back in the city. He answered O'Neill's question honestly. 'I'm a city man, so I guess that's what I will do. Why do you ask?'

'So as to warn you, I suppose,' O'Neill shrugged. 'The West has a way of changing people. Whether a man comes from New York, Omaha or some place else, there isn't any going back.'

They had called at five farms so far, meeting opposition but with an air of defeatism. The encounter with the old man they had just left had depressed them both.

'I don't understand what you're saying,' Gower said, though he was aware the fight with the Sioux had changed him.

O'Neill appeared to be having some kind of dispute within himself. Then he said, 'I come from New York, the state not the city. My home is in Troy. For me the army was going to be an adventure and not a career. In my lonely times as a soldier, and there were plenty of them, I would think of the pleasant things I'd left behind. I dreamt my dreams, in which things were always just the way I left them. I got a mighty nasty jolt when I went home to find that time had not been standing still just to support my dream. Everything had moved on. Most of what I knew had gone. As I said, there is no going back.'

They rode on for a time with the steady thudding of the hoofs of their horses as a backdrop to the new silence between them. Then Gower heard himself say, 'My dream died before I left New York.'

'Then rope yourself another dream, pronto,' O'Neill advised. 'A man can't ride through life without a trail to follow.'

'What about you, O'Neill, are you following a trail?'

Apparently regretting having given so much of himself already, O'Neill didn't answer directly. 'The point I was making, Gower, is that we've had it easy up to now. But most of these farming folk are going to fight the railroad so as to hang on to their past, their memories.'

This prophecy of O'Neill's came true less than an hour later when the valley widened out. The rich soil was black and grain fields rippled like green oceans. The building they headed towards was not like the sod huts they had called at earlier; it was a spacious cabin made from cottonwood logs from along the edges of the hills Gower and O'Neill had ridden through. O'Neill observed in his low voice. 'We've got ourselves a deputation, Gower.'

Without counting, Gower reckoned that a couple of dozen people, women as well as men, were walking slowly to meet them. It was plain that they had been warned that Gower and O'Neill were headed their way. An enormously fat man stepped forward. With a crisp goatee that couldn't conceal his multiplicity of chins, he was an imposing figure. His dress, a frock coat fancy vest and Texas boots, gave him the appearance of a wealthy Western gentleman.

A black scowl on his face, the fat man spoke as Gower and O'Neill dismounted. 'I'm Howland Yell, the democratically and duly elected spokesman for these here farming folk.'

'I'm pleased to meet you, Yell,' Gower said politely. 'It makes it easier to deal with one man.'

'Deal?' Yell scoffed. 'There'll be no deal . . . '

'Gower, Gerald Gower.'

'Well hear this, Gower. Every man and woman you see here walked into this valley alongside their wagons, and none of us wants no new-fangled railway. Go build it somewheres else.'

'I can't do that, Yell; neither can you oppose the railway.'

'We can and we sure will,' Yell said firmly. 'We joined up together to fight the moment your dad-blamed railroad

114

began your murderous campaign to drive us off our land.'

Taken by surprise by this, Gower asked, 'What are you talking about, Yell?'

'Talking about! I'll tell you what I'm talking about. I'm talking about the two Lever brothers who farmed up near Monument Peak. Killed in their beds, they were, no more'n a week since. Their place was ransacked and their savings taken, and their milch cow shot dead.'

'I can assure you that has nothing to do with the Union Pacific,' Gower said.

Not appearing to have heard him, Yell continued, 'Three nights ago they frightened Ned Mayne so bad that he ran off from his place down by the creek trail. Left Ellie, his woman, and their little girl all alone.'

'The railroad doesn't have to resort to violence,' Gower said firmly. 'I am here to offer you good money for your land, not to use force.'

Yell's eyes, squeezed into slits by fat,

went sideways to take a look at O'Neill, his glance going to the tied-down, holstered gun before remarking, 'So you may say, Gower, but it looks to me like you brought a gunfighter along to intimidate us.'

'I am Lieutenant Liam O'Neill, United States Army,' O'Neill identified himself for the fat man.

'You don't look like no officer to me,' a disbelieving Yell said.

'Were it not for Indian trouble at the construction camp, Yell,' Gower explained, Lieutenant O'Neill would have brought a body of soldiers with him to ensure that these negotiations were carried out in a peaceful manner. That is the way that the Union Pacific does business.'

Dismissing this with a shrug, Howard Yell said, 'We've settled here. We have our homes and our livelihood, and we won't let them be taken from us.'

'The State Senate passed a bill for the construction of this railroad,' Gower pointed out.

'The State Senate's a long way from here, Gower. Too far for those laws to bother us.'

Gower corrected him. 'You are wrong, Yell. I'm acting for the Union Pacific Railway and I'm bringing those laws right here to you.'

'And we're ready for you.' It was a young farmer with a flattened nose, standing with his arm around a pregnant woman, who shouted angrily at Gower.

'I'll do the talking here, Arnold,' Yell rebuked the young farmer, then told Gower, 'Phil Arnold always is mighty touchy, Gower, but he's saying what all the others feel.'

'I would prefer negotiation to confrontation,' Gower said. He raised his voice so that every one of the group could hear. 'First let me say that I appreciate your feelings. Giving up your homes and your land is the painful part of progress, but I promise that you will all share in the railroad's prosperity. The Union Pacific wants to be friends with the people of this valley.'

'That's fine,' Yell nodded, a smile reshaping his bulging face. 'We'll be your friends from the minute you say *adios* and ride out of here.'

This made most of the others laugh, and Gower looked past Yell to caution them. 'Your land can legally be taken from you without any compensation offered. That is not what the Union Pacific wants; I am here to offer you a fair price.'

'What do you mean by a fair price?' a young, clean-cut farmer enquired.

'I can't give you a definite answer on that here and now,' Gower replied.

Turning to his people, hands spread wide in a what-did-I-tell-you gesture, Yell came back round to face Gower. 'You won't give a definite answer now or any other time.'

'That's not true, Yell. Each case will need to be agreed on its merits. You wouldn't expect me to discuss private business in public. I'm prepared to attend a meeting with you all, at a time and place chosen by you, so that we can talk this over in general. Then I will meet all of you individually to settle with you.'

'What about people like poor Ellie Mayne?' a middle-aged woman wearing a scoop bonnet called. 'Unless that cowardly Ned comes back, which ain't likely, she won't have no one to speak up for her.'

'That lady will be treated as fairly as everyone else,' Gower replied.

Howard Yell said, 'Our weapons are ploughs not guns, so you won't need to bring in troopers. I studied law before taking up farming, Gower. I preserved the rights of us all by filing certain matters with the territorial court in Askaro Bend. You will be facing just me in court.'

'The courtroom is where I prefer to do business, Yell,' Gower said to end the argument as he and O'Neill mounted up.

'Let's ride for Askaro Bend and see if we can't make you a few more enemies before bedtime,' a laconic O'Neill said when they were back on the trail.

'Having Yell handle it saves you and me a lot of riding,' Gower commented.

'I'd rather have some riding and shooting to do,' O'Neill said. 'That's straightforward; your way could drag on for years, and then there's no clearcut winner.'

'I haven't got years,' Gower spoke worriedly. 'How long do you think it will be before the construction crew get here?'

'Six months at the soonest. We'll be up to our necks in snow by then, Gower.'

'I can take care of Yell's court action within six months,' a confident Gower told O'Neill. 'Will you be staying that long?'

'I was ordered to see you through to the end,' O'Neill replied.

Dusk was settling across the valley, causing Gower to shiver a little in a wind spilling down from fading red peaks. The horses seemed to feel it, too, and he heard O'Neill speaking to his black stallion. 'Keep moving, *compadre*. Tonight you'll be eating oats and I'll be sleeping in a real comfortable bed.'

That sounded good to Gower, who had yet to settle into the outdoor life and its hardships. He asked O'Neill, 'What do you make of these two brothers being killed?'

'It's nothing special, Gower. There's been renegade bands roaming this territory since the war ended.'

'I don't want these farming folk believing that the Union Pacific is responsible for what these outlaws are doing,' Gower said worriedly. 'That'll make my job harder.'

'As soon as the threat of attacks by the Indians eases off back at the end of track, I'll move a troop through this valley and clear out the renegades,' O'Neill promised.

They were riding through spruce growth that became heavier along the banks of a stream. The trees were larger, and they were weaving through them when O'Neill dismounted and hurried to a spruce clump. A curious Gower dismounted and joined him. Slumped sprawlingly on his back on the sandy ground was a thin young man, his face ashen.

Dropping to one knee beside the man, O'Neill asked, 'Where are you hit, friend?'

'In the back . . . ' the man answered, grinning like it was a joke. A sudden paroxysm of pain stopped the injured man's speech and wiped the smile from his face.

Fetching his canteen from his horse, O'Neill came back to slip an arm under the man's shoulders and eased him up a little. The man's eyes widened with gratitude when the water went down his throat. 'Thanks, that's better,' he gasped, and a faint shade of colour came into his face.

'What's your name, friend?' O'Neill asked.

'That don't make a lot of difference

122

now, mister,' the young man said weakly. 'Just pull off my boots and I can . . . '

A fit of coughing halted his speech this time. O'Neill was about to put his canteen to the white lips again when blood erupted from the injured man's mouth. Taking his arm away, O'Neill let the narrow shoulders slump back on the ground and stood up.

'Dead?' Gower enquired.

Nodding, O'Neill scanned the area around them. 'No horse.' He looked down at the body. 'Neither does he have a gun.' Kneeling again, he took each of the dead man's hands in turn to examine them.

'One of the renegades?' Gower asked when O'Neill was back on his feet.

'It wouldn't seem so. I've never seen an outlaw without a gun, or with work-calloused hands like those our late friend has.'

'So?'

O'Neill frowned. 'Well, I'm not a gambling man, Gower, but I'd bet my next month's salary that Ned Mayne won't ever be going home again. Being shot in the back says he was running from somebody.'

Gower was shocked. He had known violent crime in New York, but the murders he had encountered had had a motive. Usually it was infidelity, sometimes robbery. But killing a young dirt-farmer, a family man, was senseless. He asked, 'Why would someone want to kill him?'

'Most probably for fun,' O'Neill shrugged. 'He sure doesn't look as if he owned anything worth taking.'

'According to Yell he had a wife and a child,' an unhappy Gower remarked. 'Had we better find out where she is and tell her?'

'No,' O'Neill shook his head. 'We'll take the body into town, then let whatever law they've got there inform the widow. He was a skinny bit of a fella. I don't reckon he weighs more than a hundred pounds, so I'll carry him across the saddle in front of me.

Give me a lift with him, Gower.'

Finding the task distasteful, Gower helped O'Neill drape the body over the black stallion that objected to the smell of blood with snorting and stamping of hoofs. O'Neill calmed the horse easily enough, but Gower couldn't fight the misery inside of himself as he thought of the woman who didn't yet know she was a widow. From experience, he could imagine her distress when she did learn that her partner in life was dead.

This was still on his mind when they rode out of the valley. Up ahead, the irregular shapes of the buildings of Askaro Bend were silhouetted by the evening sky. They turned into a lane that led to a stable. Yellowy-orange lights gleamed in several of the windows. There was a cosiness to the scene that escaped Gower.

'The wanderers are home,' O'Neill lightly remarked.

Maybe it was because they had a dead man for a companion, but rather than feeling any sense of a home-coming, Gower was engulfed by homesickness. New York seemed very far distant as they rode up to the stable. He had a really bad feeling about this town.

A small man hobbled forward to meet them, a wooden leg thudding hollowly on the planking of the boardwalk. He peered through the gloom at O'Neill, trying to discover what was different about the shape of a horse and rider. Then he worked it out, and there was no welcome in his squeaky voice.

'That fella you've got there is as cold as a wagon tyre. We don't want no dead fella in the stable. He'd spook more than half the horses.'

'Take it easy, old-timer,' O'Neill advised, getting down from the saddle to pull the body off and callously hang it over a community hitching rail. 'We'll leave our friend here until we've got our broncs fixed up. Is there a lawman in this town?'

'No, not no sheriff or marshal.' The one-legged man led them and their horses into the stable. 'Jed Hayling, the blacksmith, usually takes care of any squabbles, mostly because he's bigger and stronger than any other man about here.'

'He'll do,' O'Neill nodded. 'We want these broncs rubbed down and fed.'

'That's what you'll get, stranger, so long as you pays.'

In the dull glow of an oil lamp swinging from a rafter, Gower could see the shadowy figures of three men who were saddling up. Though a novice out West he had the impression that they were desperadoes. He was aware of O'Neill watching them intently.

'What's bothering you, O'Neill?'

'I guess I know who's been killing and raiding the farmers,' replied O'Neill, his handsome face serious in the half-light. 'One of those three about to ride out is Lee Dellinski.'

'You said that the renegades in the valley would be no problem, O'Neill.'

'That was before I knew that Dellinski was the main man,' O'Neill replied grimly.

7

Being back in the saddle again wasn't a pleasant experience for Gerald Gower. The two-day stay in Askaro Bend, during which he had spent time in the company of Mercedes Glendon, had left him with no liking for the harsh lifestyle that Liam O'Neill had instantly and contentedly returned to. Dining with the beautiful Mercedes had taken Gower back to the finer shades of the living he had known, and which he longed to soon return to. The surroundings had been nowhere near as grand as a New York hotel, but the dinner had been an elegant affair, and Mercedes charming company. Uncertain as to whether O'Neill had received an invitation, Gower thought not. Though the lieutenant didn't show his feelings, the fact that he had gone on a drinking spree that night more than suggested that he had been jealous of Gower's liaison with Mercedes. Strongly suspecting there was some kind of history between the two, Gower didn't know Mercedes well enough to ask her, and was aware that O'Neill wasn't a man to be questioned.

At the end of the evening, the giant peacekeeper Jed Hayling, to whom they had delivered the body of Ned Mayne, had felled the drunken O'Neill by clubbing him with the butt of his Colt .45 in a makeshift jail. Gower marvelled at the fact that now as they rode out into the valley, O'Neill showed no sign of having been hopelessly drunk, knocked senseless, and having left a cell just an hour or so ago. In conversation with Gower, the lieutenant had quietly mentioned that he would have revenge on Jed Hayling. Though it hadn't sounded like much of a threat Gower had come to know O'Neill well enough to be frightened for the huge blacksmith.

They were on a mission of mercy

designed to impress the farmers with whom Gower would soon be negotiating. It was Mercedes' idea that he and O'Neill ride out to Ellie Mayne's farm. After Gower had gently broken the news of her husband's death, they were to deliver two large bags of provisions. Then, to show everyone how generous was the Union Pacific, Gower was to pass over to the new widow a sum of money that the farm would probably never have earned in a couple of hundred years. Mercedes had instructed Gower that he must make it clear that this money wasn't to buy the land. This was a gift, and proper payment for the land would be made later.

This was good business, and Gower admired Mercedes for planning it. At dinner with her he had, for short periods, not exactly forgotten Lola, but his wife had been less prominent in his mind than she had been since her death. Gower wasn't sure whether to be thankful or ashamed. There was the old adage that said you couldn't live with the dead, but he felt that he owed loyalty to the woman to whom he had been married.

Realisation that O'Neill had reined up on a rocky outcrop brought Gower's mind back to Union Pacific business. He stopped his horse beside the lieutenant. Before them, the sage-green valley shimmered under a westering sun. The only sign of life was a scattering of wild animals and lazily wheeling birds. Everything looked peaceful, but Gower felt a tingling along his spine as he saw that O'Neill was raised up in the stirrups. He was turning his head this way and that, carefully scanning every inch of the valley and the rocks that were close by.

Having noticed that O'Neill had been ill-at-ease since discovering that Lee Dellinski was in the area, Gower couldn't understand why. Dellinski was a hard man, that was beyond question, but he hardly ranked alongside Johnny Starr as a fighter. Though he couldn't admire the brutal streak in O'Neill, he had to admit that his handling of the half-blood up on the ledge had been masterful.

'You expecting trouble, O'Neill?' he enquired, hoping to draw the lieutenant out on the matter of Dellinski.

'There's always trouble when Dellinski's around,' O'Neill answered. 'He reached this valley ahead of us, Gower. Think about it. He must have come through Indian Territory without the kind of trouble we had.'

'Could he have just been lucky?'

O'Neill shook his head. 'No. Nobody gets lucky with Sioux. Those redskins have kept away from Dellinski because they know what he is.'

The Indians' fear of insanity was something that Gower had also learned long ago, but could now only vaguely recall. Uncertain of his ground, he asked O'Neill, 'What is he?'

'Lee Dellinski is crazy, and that scares the redskins. Him being loco makes him dangerous for us, too. It's possible to figure out what any kind of enemy, whether red or white, is likely to do, how he will react. You can't do that with a man like Dellinski.'

'You think that he'll cause us trouble?' asked Gower.

'I know that he'll cause us trouble, Gower,' a grave O'Neill replied. 'What I should do right now is hunt Dellinski down and kill him, but to do that would be to disobey orders. I have to stay with you.'

Remembering how he had spared Dellinski back at North Platte made Gower feel guilty. O'Neill hadn't said that there would be no trouble now had he shot Dellinski back there, but Gower felt sure that it was uppermost in the lieutenant's mind.

'All we can do is wait from him to make his move,' O'Neill said glumly. He touched his spurs against the flanks of his stallion. 'We'd better ride to the widow's place.'

It was an hour later when they forded the gravelly bed of a lively stream and saw the crude cabin a quarter of a mile in front of them. As they neared, O'Neill said, 'It doesn't look as if there's anyone at home, Gower. But we'd better ride in real easy like so as not to frighten a woman who is all on her lonesome.'

This thoughtfulness coming from a rugged fighting man such as O'Neill was bewildering. Over the years Gower had met many and varied characters in New York's courts, but never had he encountered a complex personality like that of O'Neill.

He couldn't help remarking, 'You seem to be a different man today than you were yesterday, O'Neill.'

'That's because I am a different man today to what I was yesterday,' O'Neill countered enigmatically.

The homestead was well situated on a piece of land with its own spring and water-hole. There was grass to be cut for winter, but time was getting short for that now. To their left two calves and their angry mother were tangled up in buckbrush. Studying the cattle for a few minutes, O'Neill then came to an agreement with himself, saying, 'If I haze those animals out of the brush it isn't going to help her without a man around the place to tend them.'

That was sound reasoning, for the place was already taking on a look of neglect. Keeping their horses at a walking pace, they headed for the cabin. They were about ten yards away when the door opened squeakily. A young woman took one step out and stood looking at them with her chin raised defiantly. Her care-worn face held a memory of a loveliness long gone. Only the beauty of her tumbling blonde hair remained. The old dress she wore had been washed so often that the print had run. She held a baby in her right arm. It was a chubby, curly-haired girl of about ten or eleven months. The baby was held under her arm, hanging awkwardly but smiling happily.

Under the woman's other arm was a Winchester lever-action 30-30 rifle.

As he and Gower climbed slowly down from the saddle, O'Neill addressed the woman. 'There is no need to be alarmed, ma'am. I don't claim to know anything about babies, but I do know about rifles. You can't handle the little girl and that Winchester at one and the same time.'

'Are you Ellie Mayne?' Gower asked.

Not speaking, she gave Gower a who-wants-to-know steady glare, and hefted the rifle a little as O'Neill ground hitched his horse and took a step forward.

'I'm Gerald Gower of the Union Pacific Railway, and this is Lieutenant Liam O'Neill of the United States Army. I am afraid that we have brought you sad tidings.'

Both the rifle and the baby seemed to sag a little more in each of her arms. First licking a tongue over dry lips, she spoke in a husky voice. 'Sorry about the rifle.' Turning, she started back in through the door, speaking to them over her shoulder. 'I can't offer you no

137

more than home-made lemon drink, but you're welcome.'

Thanking her, Gower and O'Neill followed the woman into the cabin. With a dirt floor it was barely furnished, though tidy. Putting down the heavy rifle but still holding the baby, she poured lemon from a chipped jug into tin mugs for them.

'It's Ned, isn't it?' she enquired, her face expressionless.

Nodding, Gower said, 'I'm afraid that he's been killed.'

'Shot in the back?' she asked flatly.

'How could you know that?' Gower enquired, as he and O'Neill exchanged glances.

'Because Ned Mayne never faced up to anyone or anything in his life,' she said with a harsh, mirthless chuckle. 'I am sorry that he's dead, the way I'd regret the death of anyone, but he was no use to either me or our child when he was alive, so I can't pretend to grieve.'

'At least you are honest.' Gower,

taken aback by her cold reaction, tried to make it sound like a compliment.

'Too honest, Ned always complained.' Ellie Mayne placed the child on a rickety table, a supporting hand on the chubby shoulders. 'He blamed me for riling those outlaws who rode up on us. Ned ran off when things turned nasty.'

'Were there three of them?' O'Neill asked.

'Yes.'

'Were they wearing army uniform?'

'Maybe,' Ellie Mayne shrugged. 'I couldn't rightly tell.'

'Did they hurt you, ma'am?' an anxious Gower enquired.

Surprised and apparently touched by his concern for her, she looked at Gower for a long moment. 'No, they took off after Ned. But the dark-skinned ugly one said that they'd be back. But I can take care of little Hettie and myself. When you've drunk your drinks you can go.'

'As well as to bring you news of your

husband, we came here on business,' Gower said. 'You've probably heard that the railroad will be coming through this valley.'

An indifferent nod confirmed that Ellie Mayne had heard. 'They are welcome to it.'

Taking a package from his pocket containing the money Mercedes had given him, Gower placed it on the rickety table. 'We've brought you provisions, and the Union Pacific Railway wants you to have this money.'

'Why pay me?' she asked, though poverty was making her eye the bulging package. 'There's nothing to stop the railroad from just taking this place.'

'We don't do business that way,' Gower told her. 'This money isn't payment for your farm — '

'Farm?' she interrupted him cynically. 'This place was worth just eight dollars.' Lifting the child up under one arm again she walked to a slanting shelf to reach for a small tin. Showing them that the tin was empty, she said. 'Our last eight dollars was in this can, and those desperadoes took that. Now, mister, this place isn't worth a single cent.'

'You'll be paid a fair price, just as every other landowner in the valley will,' Gower assured her.

'Together with that,' O'Neill said, pointing to the money on the table, 'the money for this place will make it easy to move out.'

Hugging the child to her, Ellie Mayne gave a brief, brittle laugh. 'Easy to move out? We have nowhere to go, no one to go to.'

Affected by her genuine despair while admiring the courage that kept her from tears, Gower heard O'Neill say, 'But you'll have to leave before snow starts falling, ma'am. You and the baby could never survive a winter here.'

'We could take you into Askaro Bend,' Gower offered.

'That place; a woman alone with a child?' Ellie Mayne shook her head. 'We'll be safer here.'

That didn't seem likely to Gower, and he said so to O'Neill as, after he had promised Ellie Mayne that they would soon be returning to buy her land, they were riding back to town. He asked, 'What if Lee Dellinski and his men go back there like he threatened to?'

'If he does, then when we next return to that cabin we'll find a dead woman and a dead child.'

Though his companion had spoken the words calmly, hearing them chilled Gower to the bone. The thought of any woman and baby alone and at the mercy of a madman in this wilderness appalled him, but he felt it all the more keenly because that woman was Ellie Mayne. For all her dire situation and her destitution, life hadn't beaten her. Ellie was not cowed but still proud. There was something special about her that made it difficult to understand how she came to be in this valley with the kind of man Ned Mayne had been. He put that sort of pondering out of his mind to concentrate on what could be done to help her.

'Maybe we should go back and take Ellie Mayne to Howland Yell and the others so they could take care of her,' Gower suggested.

O'Neill immediately dismissed the idea. 'I never took you for a romantic, Gower. Ellie Mayne is a real attractive woman, I'll grant you that, but this isn't New York. Life is tough out here and you'll find plenty of folk in real need of help. You can't help all or even one of them. We're here to do a job, so let's get on with it.'

That made sense, and Gower knew it. However, the others O'Neill had spoken of were anonymous, people he had never met, had never known, and probably would never know. The fact that he had spent time with Ellie Mayne made it impossible for him to stop worrying about her.

They were skirting the base of a brushy hill when O'Neill spoke tersely. 'Get ready to hit the dirt, Gower.'

'What's up?'

'Those large boulders to the left there, at the entrance to that narrow canyon,' O'Neill answered. 'Someone there's got a rifle trained on us.'

'Dellinski?'

'Could be. It doesn't make a lot of difference who it is when they are looking down the sights of a rifle at you.'

Saying no more, O'Neill rode on ahead of Gower. With a high rocky wall on their right, a row of high boulders on their left shielded them for a while from the concealed gunman. It was when O'Neill emerged from this protection that a gunshot boomed out, setting up echoes that rattled around the boulders. Confused by the sounds, Gower saw the splintering impact of a rifle shell on the cliff wall close to O'Neill's head. Dismounting swiftly, O'Neill, blood pouring down his face from where slivers of rock had laid open his cheek, yanked his Springfield rifle from its boot.

Forgetting O'Neill's earlier advice, Gower remained in the saddle as his horse brought him out to where the rifleman had a clear view of him. Leaping up from where he had been crouching behind a boulder, O'Neill grabbed Gower's arm and pulled him out of the saddle as another shot rang out. The echoes started up again, and Gower heard another sound close by. It was a long, hollow whistling that he couldn't identify.

Now crouching beside O'Neill behind the protection of the boulder, Gower realized what the sound was as he saw his horse sinking to its knees. It was the last breath of the animal that had taken the bullet intended for him. The horse was trying to get up, but one foreleg was doubled grotesquely under its body.

'It's a long walk back to town, Gower,' O'Neill wryly remarked, as the horse rolled on to its side, kicking convulsively.

O'Neill's black stallion had moved to

a place of safety round the edge of a cliff. It was Gower's guess that the animal had taken shelter on an order from its master. Then O'Neill nudged him and was holding out his rifle.

'I reckon there's just two of them. They've got us trapped, Gower, but we've got them in a trap as well,' O'Neill explained. 'Either them or us has to put an end to this, and I'd like it to be us.'

'What do you want me to do?' Gower asked, nervous about what was to happen.

'Take my rifle, and when I tell you, blast away at those boulders to make them keep their heads down.'

After saying this, O'Neill made a low grunting sound. Immediately, Gower heard the approaching hoofbeats of the black stallion. The horse came at a canter, not slackening its pace when it reached the boulder behind which they were crouching. Letting the animal pass, O'Neill then sprang up to vault up on its back from behind to land neatly in the saddle and, shouting 'Now' to Gower, sent the stallion towards the rocks at a gallop.

Keeping a careful eye on O'Neill so as not to risk hitting him, Gower opened up with the Springfield. He diverted his fire slightly to the left as O'Neill whirled the stallion and rode hard for the rocks at an angle. The horse took the turn at a dead run, skidding a little on some loose shale. Drawing his six-gun, O'Neill started shooting at the same time as Gower ceased firing for fear of hitting him.

Shots from a rifle came from behind the boulders, but O'Neill didn't falter in his charge. Amazed at the agility of the man, Gower watched O'Neill free one foot from the stirrups. Bringing his leg over the saddle, the lieutenant used perfect timing to leap from the horse to land sure-footedly on a jagged crag. Turning as he was landing, O'Neill fired down at someone below him.

Gower heard the hoofbeats of a fast departing horse, and saw O'Neill leaping from rock to rock with all the innate skill of a goat. Running for the rocks, Gower looked up at O'Neill, who had returned to stand on the crag, his gun now holstered.

'One of them got away, but it doesn't matter,' O'Neill reported. He pointed to below where he stood. 'I got this drygulcher.'

Gower walked round the boulder in front of him and O'Neill jumped down lightly to join him. A body was sprawled face down. Reaching out a foot, O'Neill used the toe of his boot to flip the dead man over on to his back. A pair of vacant eyes stared up at them and Gower, expecting to see one of Dellinski's outlaws, was shocked to recognize the flat-nosed features of Phil Arnold, the angry young farmer who had spoken up at the meeting with Yell.

'I said that they wouldn't give up easily,' O'Neill reminded Gower. 'It's plain they believe that if they shoot us that will be the end of the threat to their farms.'

Remembering Arnold's young and pregnant wife, Gower was filled by an immense sorrow. When he had signed on with the Union Pacific in New York he hadn't anticipated meeting violence and death at every turn. The futility of it saddened him further. Now the farm he had been ready to fight for meant nothing to Phil Arnold.

'This is a tragedy,' he said.

'You sure are right,' O'Neill agreed. 'Killing a farmer even before you start negotiating is a black mark against the Union Pacific.'

'But we had no choice, O'Neill; Arnold tried to kill us.' Gower regarded what O'Neill said to be preposterous.

Pointing to where a tiny, distant dust cloud was growing even smaller up the valley, O'Neill warned, 'That's not the way he'll be telling it when he gets back to Yell and the others.'

8

'That's better'n any of us had expected,' Howland Yell admitted.

He was sitting at a table with Gower in Askaro Bend's Kingsize Saloon. Outside the wind had changed to north-easterly, bringing silent, sifting snowflakes that were blanketing the hillside in the dusk of evening,

Though not a man given to self-praise, Gower was pleased with the progress he had made in three short days since returning to the town. The first difficulty to overcome had been the shooting of Phil Arnold. Yell had ridden into Askaro Bend to express the collective anger of the farming community. But, using all of the persuasive eloquence learned during countless court appearances; Gower had eventually convinced the farmers' spokesman that Arnold had

150

attempted to kill O'Neill and himself.

Since then Gower's negotiations had been boosted by the arrival of O'Neill's soldiers. On the edge of town the troopers were smartly putting up tents and driving in picket pins for their horses. It was a spectacle that took the fight out of Howland Yell. The show of military might made him realize that it would be futile to resist the railroad, and the generous offer Gower had just made appeared to be the decider for Yell, who did a double check by asking a question.

'You say the railroad will pay us thirty-five dollars an acre, Gower?'

'Twenty-five to thirty-five dollars depending on the land. That's what I said, Yell,' Gower replied, qualifying his offer.

Though aware that the Union Pacific wanted to move swiftly into the valley with a minimum of trouble, Gower considered that sort of money per acre to be too high. But it made his job easier, so he kept his opinion to himself.

'I've found you to be a straight, fair man, Gower. Taking all things into consideration,' Yell said, pursing lips that were disproportionately thin in his fat face, 'I would personally accept your offer right this very moment, but I have to consult all the others.'

'When will you be able to give me an answer, Yell?'

'We are all gathering at my farm in the morning,' Yell replied, doing some calculations in his head before adding, 'So I can be back here with you late tomorrow afternoon.'

A pleased Gower accepted this with a nod. 'I will be meeting Miss Glendon of the Union Pacific this evening. I think that I will be safe in reporting that you are in favour of the railroad's offer.'

'I am, but I must emphasize that it is on a personal level,' Yell said.

'Don't worry, I won't commit you in any way,' Gower assured the farmer.

The two of them parted with a

friendly hand-shake that neither man would have believed possible when they had first met.

At eight o'clock that evening Gower was elated when he joined Mercedes for dinner at Molly McCain's restaurant. They had trudged through ankle-deep snow and falling flakes that had thickened as night approached. The slippery conditions gave her an excuse to take his arm, something that they both felt comfortable with. There were few vacant tables, and a marimba band added Spanish music to an already pleasant atmosphere. Wanting her to share his delight at the pending deal, Gower broached the subject as soon as they were seated.

'I don't want to pre-empt the issue, Mercedes, but I feel sure that by this time tomorrow the farmers will have unanimously accepted our offer,' he informed her with a smile.

Expecting Mercedes to be overjoyed, he was puzzled by her muted response. Sipping her drink slowly, she kept her eyes averted. This worried him because in the short time he had been back in Askaro Bend they had become what he regarded as extra to good friends. In his younger days in New York, their relationship would have been described as a 'walking out' one. She had made a confession to him that Liam O'Neill and she had once been close. Before a romance had time to develop between them, however, her father, not wanting his daughter involved with a lower-rank army officer, had ordered O'Neill to keep away from Mercedes. This explained O'Neill's underlying dislike of Samuel Glendon.

In her honest way she assured Gower that she no longer felt anything for Liam O'Neill. Banishing a suspicion that had plagued him, Gower had found it easy to accept her word. But she was different this evening, and it took her a long time to start to speak. When she did, her eyes didn't meet his.

'This transcontinental railroad dream began on borrowed money, Gerald,' she said in a subdued voice. In the unexpected way of many people from wealthy families, Mercedes had the look of someone to whom trouble was no stranger. 'At the present moment the Union Pacific Railway finances are precarious. What with construction obstacles to overcome, the heat of the desert, bad weather, a shortage of supplies as well as attacks by Indians, costs have risen alarmingly. It now seems likely that we are to face a revolt by unpaid railroad workers.'

Fearful of what she was leading up to, Gower asked, 'Am I right in thinking that you are about to tell me something that I'm not going to like, Mercedes?'

'I am afraid that it does,' she nodded glumly. 'This is not my doing, Gerald. It is simply a case of me being told to inform you that the offer to the farmers has to be revised, downwards.'

'By how much, Mercedes?'

Now that Howland Yell had been told the top figures, Gower was convinced that the farmers' leader wouldn't agree to a cut of even one dollar an acre. Feeling betrayed by the Union Pacific that had let him go into extensive negotiations before weakening his power to deal, Gower was angry.

'Quite drastically, I regret to say,' she replied evasively.

'How drastic?'

'My father has been told by Thomas Durant that the Union Pacific can pay no more than two dollars and fifty cents an acre, that is a flat payment for everyone right across the valley.'

Stunned by this, Gower made no response. The railroad had placed him in an impossible situation. If he went back to Howland Yell with this revised offer he would lose face completely. Neither would any self-respecting farmer be prepared to move off his land for so paltry a sum. Though the army presence was increasing in numbers hourly and a Major Haslett had taken command because Liam O'Neill no longer had sufficient rank, the settlers in the valley would have no option but to fight to keep their land. Gower couldn't bring himself to contemplate the likely extent of the bloodshed that would result.

In a despairing mood he ate the meal without tasting it, and carried on a polite but detached conversation with Mercedes without knowing what either of them was saying. When he was walking Mercedes back to her hotel, their heads down as they were buffeted by a snow-packed wind, she querulously questioned him.

'Will you continue your work here, Gerald, or go back to New York?'

That was a question he had asked himself since Mercedes had given him the bad news, and he was still awaiting an answer. Hoping that replying to her would help him decide what to do, he said, 'I'm not sure that there is anything I can do here now, Mercedes. Further negotiations with the farmers are out of the question.'

'Please try,' she pleaded. 'My father has great faith in you. I heard him saying to Thomas Durant last night that the only chance the railroad has of moving into this valley peacefully rests entirely on you.'

'I am a simple lawyer, Mercedes, not a miracle-worker.'

They stopped outside her hotel. The chill of the night bit to their bones and sapped their vitality. Huge snowflakes battered her face as she looked up at him. 'Will you try, Gerald, for me? I realize that I am being selfish and that you have your own life to live, but I guess that I am asking you to stay more for my own sake than that of the Union Pacific Railway Company.'

Surprised that he was still young enough at heart to be flattered, Gower reached out to gently squeeze her upper arm. 'Whatever I decide to do, Mercedes, will be because of you and not for the Union Pacific.'

Biting at her bottom lip, leaving teeth marks in it she said pensively. 'But I do realize that you have been pushed into an unenviable position, Gerald, and I will fully understand if you decide it is impossible to continue with the railroad.'

'I'll go so far as to meet Howland Yell again tomorrow evening, and take it from there,' he replied.

That was the only commitment Gower was prepared to make in the circumstances. Seeing the hope that it brought to her eyes, and personally having absolutely no hope of success himself, he regretted making Mercedes what was a half promise.

They parted with a long, lingering look but not exchanging another word. Watching her go, slightly hunched over in the biting wind, he tried but failed to establish any similarity between her and Lola, He pondered on whether the vast difference between two women, one living, the other dead, was a good or bad thing in these circumstances.

Half an hour later, he had joined Liam O'Neill in the saloon and found himself asking the lieutenant's advice on the subject of the farmers. Not in uniform, O'Neill was wearing his buckskin outfit and drinking heavily. The long, broad room with its hard-packed earthen floor and its monstrous hewn-log bar, was crowded and rowdy. Gower got the impression that O'Neill was looking for trouble, just the way he had been when they had first met in New York.

But the lieutenant listened intently to what Gower had to say about the Union Pacific reneging on payment to the farmers. It seemed to be something that the soldier had anticipated.

Nodding sagely, O'Neill asked, 'What other reason would there be to move so many troopers and Major Haslett into Askaro Bend?'

'You mean that the railroad intends to drive out the farmers?'

'That's about the cut of it,' O'Neill said.

This didn't make sense to Gower. He couldn't understand why the Union Pacific had gone to so much trouble to engage his services and make the farmers such a generous offer. He voiced his doubts to O'Neill. 'I can't see them using force. Why change things when everything was going well?'

'Money is a funny thing, Gower,' O'Neill said cynically. 'Whether it's too much or a lack of it, everything gets altered. It seems like the farmers are going to get a rough deal. Job Haslett isn't my kind of officer. He's a mean-minded cuss.'

'You think he was selected purposely?' Gower enquired.

'I'm sure that he was. Haslett's a cruel son-of-a-bitch, and the farmers have only one hope.'

'What's that?'

'Haslett is a physical weakling who has neither strength nor vitality,' O'Neill said. 'He would be unfit for this life even in summer. The weather's getting pretty rough out there right now, and I don't reckon he will be able to survive for long in it.'

'What would happen if he didn't?'

'Maybe I could hold off the military

to give you another chance,' O'Neill suggested. He looked sympathetically at Gower. 'None of this is what you wanted, is it? What are you going to do?'

Shrugging, Gower replied, 'I'm not sure yet. I'm to meet Howland Yell tomorrow evening.'

'No, you're not.' O'Neill shook his head vehemently. 'Haslett has his orders. We're riding out into the valley at dawn and you're going with us.'

'Why do they want me to go along, O'Neill?'

'So that it looks good. You make the farmers an offer of money while Major Haslett tells them the alternative is that the army starts shooting and torching their homes. That way it looks as if they are given a choice.'

Appalled, Gower was determined to go along and possibly help the farmers in some way. He bought O'Neill and himself another whiskey, saying, 'We'd better make this the last tonight.'

'Not me,' O'Neill said, as he raised

his glass. 'I can't ride out of here tomorrow without settling a score with Jed Hayling.'

This struck Gower as stupid, and he said so. 'What good does looking for trouble do you?'

'Understand this,' O'Neill said softly. 'I've got hate churning inside me, but I can't hit back at the army, or Thomas Durant and Samuel Glendon. I have to smash something tonight so as to be able to face tomorrow.'

There was no logic whatsoever in this, but Gower had no time to mentally digest O'Neill's odd theory. The door swung open and the massive, bearded Jed Hayling stepped in. A bunch of six of his disciples came with him, staying back a respectful distance from the big man. Standing just inside the saloon, Hayling tilted his head back and scanned the place. He carried a shotgun in his huge right hand. This was one of the nightly rounds made by Askaro Bend's unofficial guardian of the peace. His dark eyes flicked over

O'Neill and Gower, dismissing them both.

Leaving Gower's side, O'Neill walked over nonchalantly with almost painfully slow strides to stand facing Hayling, who was a head taller and perhaps a hundred pounds heavier than him. A smiling O'Neill spoke softly, almost in a friendly manner.

'Well, well. The self-appointed town marshal. Any trouble in Askaro Bend tonight Hayling?'

Just about every activity in the saloon ceased. Many there had good reason to fear the giant blacksmith. The support of most of the crowd seemed to be with O'Neill, but it was support that was heavily laden with sympathy. No one there doubted the eventual outcome of a challenge to Jed Hayling.

'No trouble so far, O'Neill, and I don't expect there to be.'

'You never can tell, Hayling,' O'Neill mused in the same low voice. 'There's always the chance that someone whose head you cracked open when he wasn't looking, might come looking for revenge.'

'Anyone's welcome to take a chance at any time,' Hayling offered calmly. 'But you are an officer, Lieutenant O'Neill, and you would do well to remember that, and start behaving like an officer.'

'I'll go back to being an officer in the morning,' O'Neill said gravely. 'But tonight I'm going to take that shotgun off you, Hayling, and wrap it round your thick neck.'

A concerted gasp whispered around the room. Gower considered taking a step backward to put a gap between O'Neill and himself. He abhorred violence of any kind, and his persistent dislike of O'Neill was strengthened by the lieutenant's habit of starting trouble. If by some unlikely fluke he was able to down Hayling, then O'Neill would have his half-dozen ruffian followers to deal with. Jed Hayling's massive shoulders started a slow hunching forward, and corded veins started gathering under the skin of his ham-like hands and thickly bearded throat.

'You have a real problem, O'Neill. You've got too much mouth and not enough sense.'

'If you had the guts,' O'Neill retorted, 'you could shut my mouth for me and knock out what little sense I have.'

Unable to believe that he was being taunted by a much smaller man, the giant Hayling turned to look at his men, then whirled back to face O'Neill. Massive shoulders hunching forward again, he warned, 'I don't want to have to kill you, O'Neill.'

Before he had finished the sentence, Hayling's powerful right hand swung in a lightning haymaker. The bunched fist never reached its target. To the astonishment of the crowd, O'Neill swayed his body a little to let the punch slide by him. Then he threw a left hook with adder-striking swiftness and the lifting force of a kicking mule. It was an explosion of dynamite, hard and flat against the broad point of Hayling's bearded chin. The smacking thud of it made it seem that every muscle in Hayling's neck was tearing loose.

The towering man-mountain was being carried backward by the force when another terrific punch caught him hard against the point of his jaw. Hayling went crashing to the floor at the feet of his astonished men.

Bawling like an enraged bull, he came up at an incredible speed. His huge head was drawn into his shoulders and his dark eyes two angry streaks in his bearded face as he lunged at the bobbing, weaving, taunting figure in front of him. With a confident snarl he unleashed another haymaker. But again he was caught with two jarring punches, one to the chin and the other to the jaw. A grunt escaped from Hayling as he was slammed back against a wall. Then he steadied himself and he was rushing in again, determined to hammer down the smaller man who was punishing him.

This time Hayling employed a certain amount of caution. He weaved and bobbed, his big body darting from side to side in imitation of O'Neill. But the imitator is never as good as the imitated. A vicious right and a lifting left caught the giant to send him reeling backwards. O'Neill closed in to slam a right hook flat on Hayling's mouth.

Roaring like a maniac, the giant went down on all fours, his head wagging from side to side, blood dripping from his ruined face on to the floor. Then he rolled over to lie like a log in the dust blowing foaming blood from his broken mouth and bleeding lips.

Recovering from their shock, Hayling's men sought to avenge their hero. Catching a hold of Hayling's shotgun by the barrel, one of them swung it to catch O'Neill across the back of the head with the stock. The lieutenant fell on to both knees, and another Hayling man delivered a kick to his chest that sent him on to his back. They were all moving forwards; eager to stamp on the fallen O'Neill, when Gower sprang into action.

Grabbing one man by the hair from behind, he smashed his face into the rough wood of the bar. Rewarded by the sound of breaking bones and sinew, Gower pulled the head back and smashed it on the bar once again before releasing the man, who fell to the floor. Using a shoulder charge to knock aside a man who was kicking the inert O'Neill, Gower was conscious of something inside himself wanting to take over.

Surrendering to this strange feeling, he felt like a spectator rather than a participant as he threw a right-hand punch that twisted the head in front of him alarmingly. That man went down, and Gower weighed into another as a groggy O'Neill took handholds on the bar to pull himself to his feet. A punch from an iron-hard fist caught Gower on the side of his face, sending him crashing into O'Neill.

'Whose side are you on?' the

lieutenant asked jokingly, proving that he had recovered by dropping a man with a left-hand punch that cracked like a whip.

Standing back to back, with Gower discovering that fighting came naturally to him, they gradually got the better of an opposition that outnumbered them. When the last man went down, they rested their backs against the bar, elbows on the counter, breathing hard, bloody but far from bowed.

Looking down at the mashed faces of the men lying at their feet O'Neill clapped Gower on the back, his bruised and swollen face managing a grin as he said, 'Now I'm ready to face tomorrow.'

A bewildered Gower made no response at first. Then he found that he was feeling happier than he had for a very long time. It was as if he had suddenly become whole. His face felt tight and painful, and his knuckles ached, but there was a wonderful feeling surging up inside him.

'Do you know, I think I am, too,'

Gower laughed.

A smiling O'Neill offered his hand. 'Put it there, Gerald.'

'I'm proud to do so, Liam,' Gower shook the hand warmly.

An arm around each other's shoulders in friendship and for support, they walked unsteadily from the saloon together.

9

In the cold bleakness of the next morning, with Major Job Haslett riding in front like Caesar ahead of his legions, they got under way. A low mist hung over the camp, over the town, over the trees. The icy air made breathing difficult. Back in uniform, Liam O'Neill was once more every inch a military officer, despite his good looks being disfigured. His left jaw was swollen grotesquely, and his blackened left eye was partially closed. Gower's own face was causing him discomfort. The sense of comradeship with O'Neill that had come so suddenly the previous night, somehow fortified Gower for the difficulties that lay ahead. O'Neill had half joked that he had 'become a fighting man overnight'. That could be true, as for the first time since coming out West Gower was at one with the environment. He felt really alive. Though as a civilian he was separate from the troop, he felt a sense of pride, a sense of belonging.

Haslett, a small, incredibly thin man with illness stamped on a prematurely lined face, had earlier briefed his men. They would, he said, be facing civilians who may well be every bit as hostile as the Sioux. This meant that the farmers would be dangerous.

'If the order is given to fire,' the major said at the end of his talk, 'then shoot to kill.'

That had chilled Gower. It was plain that Haslett, a soldier through and through, had dismissed any possibility of a settlement with the farmers.

The mist was gradually lifting and the way became brighter. But it remained cold and Gower huddled inside the heavy coat that O'Neill had got from the stores for him. O'Neill rode just in front of Gower, a heavily built sergeant at his side. The snow on the ground was crisp with ice, creaking and cracking under the horses' hoofs. The mist remaining formed dazzlingly bright-white outlines round the trees.

In front of them the sky first turned purple and then a heavy black. A wind that had been just strong enough to occasionally dislodge light whirls of snow from the tips of branches was stiffening.

Less than an hour later they were pushing through a blizzard. A sixty-mile-an-hour wind was blowing and with the temperature well below zero, Gower had never been so cold. A great deal of snow was falling. Gower was just able to make out O'Neill ride off past the column of troops. A short while afterwards he came back, riding up to Gower to shout above the roar of the wind.

'I tried to persuade Major Haslett to let us take shelter, Gerald, but he wants to press on.'

Gower had difficulty finding his voice to shout back. 'What do we do?'

'Obey orders and carry on. This is the army,'

With that O'Neill moved off, leaving Gower to wonder whether his last words had been spoken sarcastically. Gower became so numbed by the cold that at first he didn't realize that the wind was dropping fast and it had stopped snowing.

The column of troops halted. In a white world, O'Neill was signalling him forward, and Gower joined O'Neill and the sergeant in a ride past the stationary troopers to the head of the column. A wood was facing them that would provide shelter and fuel for fires in the fast-approaching night. A snow-plastered Haslett sat astride his horse, the right arm he had raised to halt his troop still held aloft. Gower could see that the wizened face had purpled with the cold.

'He saw sense and called a halt at last,' O'Neill muttered, as he rode up to his superior officer. Then he cursed. 'The old fool!'

Gower called, 'What's happened, Liam?'

'Major Haslett's dead. I knew this would be too much for him.'

Liam O'Neill then showed his qualities as a commander. He became a super-efficient officer, rapping out orders that his men jumped to obey. 'Troopers Male and McKenzie, come forward and take the major down from his horse.'

Two young troopers dismounted and did as they were told. It was plain that they found handling the corpse of their commanding officer distasteful. Finding it eerie himself to see the stiff body of Haslett held upright, his right arm still raised in an eternal signal, Gower sympathized with the young soldiers.

'We can't get the major's arm down, sir,' one of them reported. 'It's frozen.'

'Break it,' O'Neill ordered brusquely.

'But, sir . . . '

O'Neill raised his voice: 'Break it soldier.'

Face averted, one of the troopers embraced the dead officer while the other grasped the raised arm with both hands and pulled down. At first nothing happened. Gower could feel tension building up among the still mounted troopers. Then there was a mighty crack that was louder than the report of a rifle. The trooper who had been pulling on the arm fell face down in the snow as it suddenly came down. O'Neill issued orders to the sergeant.

'We'll make camp in the woods tonight, Sergeant Rearden. Form a wood-chopping party and get some fires going. Tell the men that we will be returning to camp in the morning.' He turned to Gower. 'Do you agree that we turn back, Mr Gower?'

Relieved that the death of the major could well mean a re-think on moving the farmers out of the valley by force, Gower replied, 'I have no objection, Lieutenant O'Neill.'

O'Neill spoke to the sergeant. 'Have the men dismount and make camp,

Sergeant. Post four sentinels' — looking around he pointed in four separate direction — 'north, south, east and west.'

'Begging your pardon, sir,' the burly sergeant frowned. 'The hostiles never come in this far.'

'I'm not thinking about Indians, Sergeant,' O'Neill snapped. 'There are renegades in the area. At the start of winter they would risk anything for the supplies on our pack-horses.'

'Sir,' the sergeant saluted before walking stiff-backed to yell orders at the troopers.

When the camp had been set up, Gower sat beside O'Neill at one of the four fires that were burning on each side, with a tunnel of warmth in between. They were eating a hastily cooked but welcome hot meal, when O'Neill tendered some advice. 'When you bed down in your blankets tonight Gerald, make sure that you cover your head as well as your body. It makes the difference between sleeping or lying awake shivering all night.'

'Thanks, I'll remember that,' Gower said.

Standing up, O'Neill went to where Sergeant Rearden was beckoning. After an inaudible conversation with Rearden, O'Neill's usually expressionless face looked anxious as he returned to hunker beside Gower and report, 'One of the sentries has spotted three riders heading south-west, Gerald.'

Gower enquired, 'Which means?'

'Lee Dellinski has to be one of the three,' O'Neill said evenly. 'There's another storm brewing, and getting caught in a northern blizzard is no joke. They'll be seeking somewhere to hole-up. There's only one farm south-west of here, Gerald.'

'Ellie Mayne's place!' Gower was aghast.

'You've got it. Dellinski's been there before, so he's likely to go back.'

'What can we do, Liam?'

'I can do nothing,' an unhappy O'Neill replied. 'If I send as much as one man after them I'd be court-martialled and spend the rest of my life in an army prison. And you don't know enough about out here to survive one hour on a night like this.'

'Maybe so, but I've got to try,' a determined Gower said, thinking of Ellie and her child. 'I roughly know the direction, and it should be easy to follow their tracks.'

'If it doesn't snow again,' O'Neill remarked.

'What will I need, Liam?'

O'Neill answered wryly, 'A supply of food and a rifle, both of which I can provide, and a whole heap of luck which is something I can't help with. I fear for that woman, too, Gerald, but I have to advise you not to go. You wouldn't have an outside chance of surviving the elements, without coming up against Dellinski.'

'I don't have a choice.' Gower was adamant.

'Well, in that case,' O'Neill said worriedly, 'if you do make it to Ellie's place, shoot Dellinski and his men on sight. Remember that it's kill or be killed.'

That prospect daunted Gower, as he listened to O'Neill's advice. 'This moon will only light your way for the next three hours or so, Gerald. Stop for the night then. I'll have the troopers chop some wood for a fire when you bed down. Have you still got that six-gun?'

From outside of his heavy coat, Gower patted the bulge made by the gun. 'Yes.'

'Then keep your gun and rifle real close.'

These instructions ran through Gower's mind two hours later when night had settled down dark, damp and thick with cold. He chose a hollow to bed down in for the night. A deadly, mist poured into it and rose among the trees until he could only see the ones near at hand. He swiftly built a fire and settled down in his bedroll. Four strategically spaced fires were best, O'Neill had explained, but were too extravagant needing more wood than one man could either carry or collect.

Sleep eluded him. Mind racing, he marvelled at how his life had altered so dramatically in so short a time. He realized now that he had earlier been in no position to judge O'Neill. The lieutenant had lived a much harsher life than he had; a life that Gower had known nothing about, What he was certain that he would never accept was that O'Neill had been capable of killing the Sioux boy in cold blood. His thoughts then became muddled and he must have drifted off to sleep.

Awaking suddenly, Gower instantly sat up straight. The fire had died down but was throwing out a good deal of heat. A struggling dawn was aided in lifting the darkness by reflection from the snow. Throwing the remainder of his wood on the fire, he squatted and ate some of the dried meat O'Neill had ordered a trooper to pack for him. Then he secured the bedroll behind the saddle, and led the horse up out of the hollow.

Still on foot he crossed another hollow, slipping on the ice that crusted a frozen stream. Walking up a slope to the next crest he swung stiffly up into the saddle. He rode through brush, the naked branches and slender stems of which were encased in ice. The cold of it brushed against his clothes and set him shivering.

Then he was out in the open. A great white expanse stretched before him. He was uncertain that he was heading in the right direction until he came upon snow churned up by the hoofs of three horses. The tracks went on ahead of him as far as he could see, as clearly marked as a well-charted trail on a map.

Tired by the cold, he tracked Dellinski and his two men all day. Sooner than he had calculated, he topped a rise to see Ellie Mayne's humble dwelling in the near distance. There was a scarlet sunset behind it, vivid with a beautiful blending of colours. The sunset faded fast to be replaced by the ghostliness of the night, a strange light, with the still stranger mist in the trees making Gower feel hollow and suddenly agonizingly home-sick. He fervently wished himself back in the known streets of New York. The surroundings and the scene before him was too unearthly for him to cope with.

Then he recalled Ellie and her plight. Gower regained control of himself. The tracks went on directly to the cabin. It would be foolish to ride in even under the cover of dawn, so Gower left his horse tied to a tree. Carrying his rifle, he moved off carefully on foot.

Keeping to cover as much as possible, he approached the cabin in an arc. A dull orange light glowed in the single window and a thin spiral of smoke rose from the chimney. The tracks went right up to the door. His heart quickened to notice that the three tracks led away again. Relieved, Gower felt certain that Dellinski and the others had simply stopped to rob Ellie of provisions before moving on again.

Needing to be sure, he walked in the tracks of the three horses until they led into the beginning of a forest at the top of the hill. Satisfied, he retraced his steps to stand facing the cabin. Bringing his rifle up to the hip in readiness, he discovered that his gloved finger was too large to go in the trigger guard. Needing to be prepared before calling to Ellie, he took off the glove. Within seconds, his hand was so cold that it was useless. Tucking the rifle under his arm, he searched his coat pocket for a clasp knife. Slicing off the forefinger of the glove, he put it back on. His bare finger ached with the cold, but he would be able to work the trigger with it.

The situation and everything else was alien to him. All around was a howling waste of desolation. Uncertain as to what to do next, he tried to imagine what action Liam O'Neill would take if in his position. Such imagery was pointless, because the contrast between his upbringing and lifestyle and that of O'Neill was too great.

Gower knew that to delay further was unwise. His feet and hands were freezing. A fine sleet had begun to lash his face savagely and his eyelids and lashes were so coated with ice that he had difficulty in seeing. Forcing himself, he walked forwards, calling, 'Ellie, are you there? It's me, Gerald Gower from the Union Pacific Railway,'

The flailing sleet-packed wind caught his words and changed things somehow so that it didn't sound like his voice. Gower was about to shout again when there was a cracking sound as the ice broke around the frame as the door was slowly opened. Gower was relieved to see Ellie Mayne standing there, a blanket wrapped around the child held in her arms.

'It's all right Ellie,' he called reassuringly.

She stood back to allow him to squeeze past her in the doorway. Smoke from the fire irritated his eyes for a moment. Blinking rapidly, he heard the flailing of the wind shut off behind him as Ellie closed the door. Then an icy-cold muzzle of a gun pressed against his cheek and the rifle was tugged from his hand. Turning his head, he saw that the chisel-faced Lee Dellinski was holding the gun against his head. The renegade's lips parted to put long, yellow teeth on display in a mirthless grin. The heavy coat he had on over his worn uniform was too small for him. Gower guessed that it had belonged to Ned Mayne.

One of Dellinski's men, unusually muscular and with a blood-red beard-covered face, had taken the rifle from him. A mass of unruly red hair hung down from under a battered brown hat. Using one hand to hitch up a pair of criss-crossed cartridge belts hung round his waist, he tossed it across the room to where a lad stood nervously. The boy, short in stature and with a body that was too slim to possess strength, clumsily caught the weapon.

'I'm sorry,' Ellie Mayne apologized unnecessarily.

She had no reason to be sorry. Dellinski had fooled him with the horse tracks in the snow. Now realizing that the horses were in the trees on the hill behind the house, Gower was acutely aware of his shortcomings in life out here in the West.

The pressure of the gun muzzle eased off from Gower's cheek. He expected Dellinski to speak. But in an incredibly swift movement, the renegade cracked Gower across the head with the barrel of his six-shooter. Stunned, Gower fell sideways, aware of the small cabin being filled by Ellie's scream and her baby's frightened crying. Crashing against a wall, he slid semi-conscious to the floor.

Holstering his gun, Dellinski came to stand over him. Reaching down, the outlaw grabbed Gower by the front of his coat and yanked him to his feet. Still holding the coat to keep the groggy

Gower upright, Dellinski punched him hard in the stomach.

The agony from the punch was too much to endure, and Gower felt himself slipping into unconsciousness. He heard Ellie shout 'Stop it! Stop it!' then Dellinski's bunched fist hit him full in the face and he knew no more.

Coming round, Gower instinctively brushed the blood from his eyes and wiped his bleeding mouth. He had been propped in a chair. Still hugging her child to her, Ellie was standing close to the fire, eyes wide in horror and sympathy. Dellinski sitting at the other side of a table, was studying him. The outlaw tensed as Ellie moved towards Gower, the child in one arm, and a cloth in her other hand. She glanced at Dellinski, who nodded grudgingly, then she came close to wipe the blood from Gower's face.

'You had to be taught who is in charge here. If it's any consolation to you, Gower,' Dellinski began to explain the beating he had given to Gower, 'you've given me a lot of pleasure. I'm a natural-born gunfighter, but there is something more intimate in fisticuffs; the personal touch, so to speak.'

Half listening to what the renegade was saying, his head back as Ellie tended his damaged face, Gower struggled to convey a message with his eyes as he fumblingly undid his coat. Seeing the handle of the six-gun protruding from his belt, Ellie understood. Her eyes flicked to where Dellinski sat with his head down, rolling a cigarette. Pretending to search for an unbloodied section of her cloth, she reached for the gun. Ellie's dextrous fingers plucked the gun from his belt and transferred it inside the blanket in which her child was wrapped.

Lighting his cigarette, Dellinski waved her away from Gower. 'That's enough. No tenderfoot from back East ever got toughened up with a woman fussing over him.' He pointed a finger at Gower. 'We are going to sit the winter out here, *compadre*. Though an unexpected guest, you are not unwelcome. If you can fetch and carry, go out there in the snow and bring in wood for the fire. You take care of me'n Red,' — he indicated the bearded man — 'and young Lennie here, through the bad months, then when the spring comes we'll decide what to do with you.'

Able to predict what would happen to him in the spring, Gower didn't intend to wait. When the opportunity came to retrieve his revolver, and he was certain that at the time he wouldn't endanger either Ellie or her little girl, he would take Dellinski and the other two by surprise.

'That's some of the rules laid down,' Dellinski was saying, as he stood up to walk across the small room to where Ellie stood, 'but the most important thing for you and this gal to remember is that it don't do to try to trick Lee Dellinski.' He held out a hand to Ellie. 'That kid will be a whole lot more comfortable without that .44 sticking in its side.'

With a helpless, hopeless glance at Gower, Ellie handed over his gun to Dellinski.

10

There was no way of telling, but Lee Dellinski had decided that it was Christmas Day. It was a time for celebration, he declared. He ordered Red to break out two bottles of whiskey that the outlaws had obviously been saving for a special occasion. Dellinski poured three drinks and passed one to an eager Red. The boy, Lennie, who would have been a good-looking kid had it not been for a flat nose that was spread too wide across his young face, reached for one of the drinks, but Dellinski pulled it sharply away from him.

Turning to Ellie and Gower, Dellinski's dismay appeared to be genuine as he exclaimed, 'Did you see that? A boy of his age wanting to drink whiskey. I ask you, what is this world coming to?' He pushed the tin mug towards Ellie.

'You drink it, Ellie.'

'No thank you.'

His mood swiftly changing, Dellinski's cold eyes were angry slits as he said, 'That wasn't an invitation, it was an order.'

Gower was distressed to watch a terrified Ellie take the mug and raise it to her lips. Her child was asleep in a makeshift cot that was no more than a wooden box. Reaching out a hand, Dellinski placed a thick forefinger under the mug to tilt it so that the liquor ran into her mouth. Things were turning ugly, but Gower tried to cling to a hope that Dellinski and Red would get helplessly drunk. If they did he would think up some scheme to put them both out of action. It wouldn't be easy, because the murderous Dellinski was sure to still be a danger when drunk, possibly more than when sober. Gower didn't see the boy as a threat. In different circumstances Lennie would probably be a nice kid.

Having been a captive, a veritable

slave, for what must have been more than two weeks now, Gower had become despondent. Dellinski had sent the boy to collect Gower's horse and put it in the rickety barn out back with their mounts. But that didn't interest Gower, who wanted to help Ellie there in the cabin, not get away.

The two men outlaws watched him carefully, and his life spent in a city put him at a disadvantage against men who had roughed it out West all of their years. Dellinski gave no indication that he remembered Gower from the incident at North Platte, but Gower was half-convinced that he did. What Gower was certain of was that he hadn't helped Ellie by attempting to come to her rescue, but doing so had doubtless cost him his job with the Union Pacific. Liam O'Neill would do his best to make things right for him with the railroad, but that wouldn't be enough. Gower's third, final, and most desolate sense of failure was that he had lost Mercedes. When the snow eventually stopped falling and the thaw set in, the Union Pacific would need to move into the valley at once. Even if he survived after the arrival of spring, Gower would never get back to the Union Pacific in time to play any part in securing the valley. Without the railway for a base, the budding relationship between Mercedes and himself could not develop.

In his lowest moments he had started to wonder if fate wasn't making decisions for him. The possibility that he was meant to spend his life here as a farmer with Ellie for a wife had occurred to him but he knew that couldn't be so. Ellie was a sweet woman, but never could she replace Lola. Mercedes was the only woman likely to at least share his heart with his dead wife, but now he would never know for sure.

Dellinski downed his mug of liquor in one long swallow. Refilling Ellie's mug and his own, he forced another drink on her. 'Happy Christmas.' He leered at her as he handed over the mug and forced her to drink. Ellie's pretty face had reddened and her tear-filled eyes were glazed. Poignantly she kept glancing towards her sleeping daughter.

'That's enough, Dellinski.'

Gower had stood up from the table when he had rapped out the words, and an enraged Dellinski stood to face him, jabbing a finger into Gower's face. 'You . . . you do not tell me what to do.'

'I'm telling you to let that woman be,' Gower said threateningly.

Apparent amusement on his hard face, Dellinski turned away from Gower. But he swung back swiftly to catch Gower a backhanded blow to the face that sent him flying backwards. Hitting the floor hard, Gower came up fighting. Though slightly drunk by then, Red was alert, tripping Gower as he lunged at Dellinski. Propelled forward by the trip and his own momentum, Gower ran straight into Dellinski's fist. The punch sent him backwards, head over heels. He landed with the back of his head smacking hard against a wall.

The noise woke the child, who began to cry loudly, and Gower, his head swimming, gathered from the look of horror on Ellie's face, that he must be bleeding freely.

Intending to pick up her daughter, Ellie was walking to the child when Dellinski stopped her. Putting a hand on each of her hips, he lifted her and stood her on the table. Bewildered, she stood where he had put her, looking anxiously towards her crying baby.

'It's Christmas, a time to have fun,' Dellinski announced. 'Dance for us, woman.'

Dellinski started up a loud but untuneful rendition of a Christmas carol, then suddenly change it to 'Turkey in the Straw'. A grinning Red started to clap his hands rhythmically, and Lennie, who slavishly and constantly copied both Dellinski and Red, joined in. A frightened Ellie didn't move a muscle. She flinched as Dellinski roared at her.

'Dance, woman, dance.'

There was still no movement from Ellie. Fearful for her, aware that her ordeal was only just beginning, Gower began to shakily ease himself up from the floor. The man and the boy quickened their clapping and Dellinski, his eyes glowing even more madly than usual, was swaying his hips in time with the new tempo.

'Dance!' he yelled again but Ellie stood with her arms wrapped round herself, her slim body shuddering.

Exasperated, Dellinski looked around him wildly. Then he drew a Colt .45 from its holster and fired all in one smooth movement. A glass jar on a shelf just above the makeshift cot shattered explosively. Glass showered down into the cot. The acrid reek of cordite filled the little cabin. The child began screaming while at the same time the hand-clapping reached an unbearable crescendo. Still on the table, Ellie cried and begged incoherently.

Spinning the six-shooter on his finger, a laughing Dellinski made several pretences at firing more shots in the direction of the cot. He yelled at Ellie above the noise, 'I aim to get me some more target practice if you don't get to dancing.'

Still crying, Ellie began a slight swaying of her body. Some distant memory of having danced as a girl gradually took her over. Now grinning in delight, Dellinski holstered his gun and moved closer to the table as Ellie began to take little dancing steps. Shadowed behind her movements was an immense terror.

Joining in with the hand-clapping, Dellinski ordered Ellie, 'Lift your skirts, woman, and flare them around like I've seen them dark-eyed *señoritas* do.'

Fear had Ellie obey, but she hoisted her skirts only a modest inch or so. Knowing that this wouldn't satisfy Dellinski and Red for long, Gower rested against the table to recover his strength. Though aware that he didn't have a chance against the two armed men, he had to try to help Ellie, even though he was certain to die in the attempt.

But he attracted Dellinski's attention by pushing himself upright. Picking up Gower's coat, angrily Dellinski came round the table to grab Gower. Opening the door, he shoved Gower out and threw his coat after him, ordering him to get wood for the fire.

Gower paused close to the corner of the cabin, which helped to turn the edge of the cutting wind. He shrugged into his heavy coat, as the door of the cabin was slammed shut. He stood disconsolately listening to the volume of hand-clapping increase inside. He trudged slowly through the snow to where the wood he had earlier been forced to cut was stacked beside the single tree that stood close to the cabin. An unidentifiable noise made him scan the snow-covered landscape. It wasn't possible that help was at hand, but he would have welcomed an attack by a band of Sioux forced by starvation to stray far from their territory. Death for

Ellie and himself would be preferable to what was happening right then.

On a ridge above him broke the silhouette of a great bull moose. Looking all snow-white in the winter light it started down the slope with enormous strides. Suddenly, the moose became aware of his presence. Halting, it looked at him with some kind of question in its black eyes. Whatever the question was, the animal answered it for itself. Shaking its head, the moose turned and walked away on stiff legs. Gower found himself ludicrously wanting to call the animal back, needing its company.

Picking up a thick piece of branch that was about a foot long, he weighed it carefully in his hand. What chance would he have if he burst back into the cabin with this as a weapon?

Such a move would be futile. Knowing that, Gower was dismissing the idea when he heard Ellie scream piercingly. No longer in any doubt as to what he must do, Gower hefted the heavy length of wood, ready to run to the cabin door, when he heard his name called softly.

'Gerald.'

Astonished, he turned to see Liam O'Neill come out from behind the tree. He wore his uniform with a heavy civilian coat over it, and was laconically saying, 'I thought that moose would spot me before you did.'

Gower glanced anxiously at the cabin, but O'Neill and he couldn't be seen from the window. Ellie's screams had lowered to a continuous wailing; a sound more harrowing than before. O'Neill was studying Gower's battered face. He smiled the sort of smile that a man usually reserves for children and women, a smile symbolic of the bond that had grown between them during their last few days together. There was no time to ask each other questions.

Passing Gower a six-shooter, O'Neill said tersely, 'Hide this in a bundle of wood, and get back in there fast. I'll wait out here. Try to get Dellinski outside. We can't risk too much shooting inside because of the woman and girl.'

Taking the gun, now filled with hope and determination, Gower quickly gathered up wood and made his way towards the cabin door. Every nerve in his body was strained taut. He was starkly aware that whatever happened in the next few minutes was down to him. It was an awesome responsibility.

At no time had Dellinski and Red regarded him as any kind of a threat, and they didn't look now as Gower opened the door and stepped inside. Red was up on the table trying to embrace a struggling Ellie, while Dellinski stood watching and laughing. The singing and enforced dancing had come to an end. For some odd reason the boy was still rhythmically clapping.

Red would have been a difficult target for a professional gunslinger as he fought with Ellie, who was just as likely as he to stop the bullet. It was far too dangerous a shot for Gower, a total novice with a handgun. But something similar to what had taken him over during the fight in the saloon once again relieved him of the need to think out a plan of action, the need to direct his limbs.

Dropping the bundle of wood, Gower fired from the hip. He saw a small black hole appear above Red's right ear just in front of the straggling long hair. For a few seconds the bearded man continued to paw Ellie, completely unaffected. Then his head tilted to the left as if he was listening to something. Holding that pose for what seemed a long time to Gower, his whole body then leaned to the left defying gravity before he toppled sideways off the table.

Dellinski immediately leapt into action, drawing his gun fast. But Gower quickly went out of the door. With Dellinski close behind him, he started to run for the nearest cover. Disaster overtook him as he slipped down on his haunches, sliding on the icy crust of the snow and knocking up a shower of it before him.

Coming out of the door, a confident Dellinski leisurely aimed his gun at the crouching, defenceless Gower. Without even the time to raise the gun in his hand, Gower accepted that this was the end. But a bullet sang through the air past him as O'Neill fired from behind the tree. The angle was wrong for an accurate shot, but O'Neill's bullet caught Dellinski in the right arm. The arm dropped uselessly, with blood pouring down over the hand and the gun that it held.

Coming up on to one knee, Gower aimed his gun at Dellinski. Even though the man was a crazy, ruthless renegade, because Dellinski was defenceless, Gower had to steel himself to shoot him. He was about to pull the trigger when Lennie dashed out of the cabin to run and stand protectively in front of Dellinski, the man he idolized.

'Shoot them, Gerald, shoot them

both,' O'Neill shouted from behind the tree.

Gower couldn't do it. The boy's fearless eyes were staring at him, challenging him to do as he wished, ready to die to save Dellinski. A crunching of the snow behind him told a relieved Gower that O'Neill had come out from behind the tree and was approaching. Together they could take the boy and the injured Dellinski alive.

Relaxing into this plan, Gower was horrified to see Dellinski, through some supreme effort, bring up his badly injured gun hand. It was plain that while using Lennie as a shield he was aiming at O'Neill. Even so, Gower hesitated. Then he fired and something instantly died inside him as he saw his bullet punch a bloody hole right in the centre of the boy's widespread nose. As Lennie fell dead, Dellinski and O'Neill fired simultaneously. Coughing blood, Dellinski doubled over, then his legs sagged and he went down on to his knees. Another cough ended in a gurgle as clotted blood erupted from his mouth and he slowly stretched out flat as he died.

Getting to his feet Gower was joined by O'Neill, who looked down at the dead Lennie and said, 'I guess you could say that we are equal partners now, Gerald.'

Understanding that O'Neill was comparing his killing of the Sioux boy with his having just shot Lennie, Gower, surprised at how strained O'Neill's voice sounded, turned to comment just as O'Neill collapsed face down on the ground. Blood seeped from underneath his prone body to rapidly stain the snow red.

Dellinski's bullet had lodged in O'Neill's chest perilously close to the heart. Ellie helped Gower get him into the cabin and make him as comfortable as possible. Gower took time out only to fetch O'Neill's horse from where he had left it in the trees on the hill. Then he and Ellie gravely debated what to do to help the unconscious O'Neill. Both of them lacked any medical knowledge, but they agreed that O'Neill would soon die if the bullet wasn't removed. But it was equally evident to both Ellie and Gower that the lieutenant was likely to die even sooner as a result of any amateur surgery that they might attempt.

But with no real option, they prepared to remove the bullet. The only knife that Ellie had was a huge carving knife with a bone handle. Gower scraped away snow behind the cabin to uncover a grinding stone Ned Mayne had once used to sharpen farming implements. Though the temperature was well below zero, Gower sweated as he ground the carving knife down until it resembled his idea of a scalpel. He next snapped three tines from a four-tined dinner fork for use as a probe, and then they sterilized the crude surgical instruments in a pan of boiling water on the wood stove.

Learning as he worked, hoping for the best, Gower probed deep into

O'Neill's chest until the tip of his improvised surgical instrument made contact with the bullet. Not sure whether he might be causing permanent damage or even killing his patient, Gower used the knife to cut flesh away to get at the bullet. As he worked, a stoic Ellie used a ripped apart blanket to clear away the blood that flowed profusely from the wound. At last Gower could see the end of the bullet when Ellie entered a cloth-covered finger into the wound to mop up the blood.

Using the probe on one side and his scalpel on the other to grasp the bullet, Gower was disheartened to discover how firmly it had embedded itself in O'Neill's body. Sweat running into his eyes, icy fingers of fear clutching at his heart, Gower very gently rocked the end of the bullet from side to side. An hour later he had released it enough to remove it but a build-up of blood swiftly created a suction that held the bullet fast.

With O'Neill now losing so much blood that he wouldn't last much longer, Gower was close to despair. But, proving how resourceful she was, Ellie pulled a pin from her long hair. With her hair tumbling freely, she straightened the hairpin before placing the end in the boiling water. Gower realized what she had in mind, and gazed at her admiringly as she came back to bend over O'Neill.

Gripping the end of the bullet tightly, Gower was ready when Ellie jabbed the pin deep into the wound to break the suction. The bullet came out so easily that he staggered backwards. Then there was no time to spare. They had to stop O'Neill's massive bleeding. Using Gower's probe, Ellie hooked from the pan a small square of blanket that she had been boiling. Holding it up with the scalpel to drain and cool, she tested the temperature of the cloth by holding it near to her face, then dropped it into O'Neill's wound, using the probe to tamp the wad in tightly to plug the wound and stop the bleeding. She then helped Gower make bandages from what remained of the blanket, and wrap O'Neill's upper body tightly.

When it was done, Ellie and Gower hugged each other in relief. Even so, they had a worrying time ahead of them. Nursing O'Neill through that first night, they were convinced several times that they had lost him. His condition stabilized in the days that followed, but Gower judged that more than a week had passed before O'Neill's eyes flickered open.

Moving weakly, he ran his hands over his bandaged chest, and the old Liam O'Neill could be detected when he remarked in a faint voice, 'I guess you'd make a better sawbones than you do a lawyer, Gower.'

'That's because you're a much better patient than you are a soldier,' Gower countered, and was rewarded by a ghost of a smile that made a fleeting appearance on O'Neill's pale face.

'I'll make you some broth.' Ellie,

delighted by O'Neill's return to con-
sciousness, stood up from beside the
bed.

Becoming aware of her presence for
the first time, O'Neill moved his head
to look up at her, and Gower told him,
'I only took the bullet out of you, Liam;
Ellie did the nursing. I don't think she's
slept since you got hit.'

Mouthing an almost silent, 'Thank
you,' O'Neill reached out and took her
hand before sliding back into unconsciousness. A pleased Ellie blushed and
tenderly placed O'Neill's hand back on
his chest before walking away.

Relieved to see O'Neill's coma
gradually change to a peaceful sleep,
Gower went over to stand beside Ellie
as she heated broth on the stove.
Having become attached to her in a
brotherly way, he wanted to find words
to prepare her for more trouble, while
at the same time not alarming her.

'He's coming on real well,' she said
with a wan smile. There were dark rings
under her eyes from lack of sleep.

Gower had constantly marvelled at the vitality that had made it possible to care for her own young daughter and the severely wounded Liam O'Neill at the same time.

'We'll get him back on his feet,' Gower promised her, but then added a caution in a low voice in case O'Neill should be awake and overhear. 'Liam's problems won't be over even when he's well again, Ellie.'

'I don't understand.'

The concentration on her pretty face as she poured broth from a pan into a bowl, somehow made her look child-like, vulnerable. Gower wanted to slip a comforting arm round her slim shoulders. Having witnessed her tremendous strength and courage, he held Ellie Mayne in the highest regard.

'Liam wouldn't have come here with the permission of the army, Ellie.'

'Does that mean that he'll be punished, Gerald?' she anxiously asked.

'Severely,' he replied, not wanting to tell her more, and not wishing to

214

contemplate what could be O'Neill's fate. During the war there had been numerous executions for desertion in both armies.

Ellie frowned worriedly. 'How can we help him?'

'I'll find out when he's a bit better,' Gower assured her.

Another ten long days passed before O'Neill awoke in the morning feeling stronger. Waiting until Ellie had patiently fed him, Gower asked O'Neill. 'What happened after I left you, Liam?'

'I took my men back to Askora Bend the next morning,' O'Neill frowned, as he struggled to recall incidents from the other side of having been seriously wounded, 'and handed over Major Haslett's body. I reported to Mercedes Glendon where you had gone, and why.'

'How did she react to that?'

Gower unsuccessfully tried to keep the intense interest out of his voice. Mention of Mercedes had reawakened a lot of feelings that had lain dormant since he had been at the cabin. It was important for him to have all the details about her, but he knew that he had to restrain his questioning.

'That's difficult to answer. Mercedes probably thought you were a gallant gentleman riding to Ellie's rescue, but she's a company girl, Samuel Glendon's daughter, and the Union Pacific favour profit over sentiment. It's my guess that in abandoning your mission here in the valley you forfeited your position with the railroad.'

'That's the way I see it,' Gower agreed with a nod.

'None of this is what you wanted is it Gerald?' O'Neill observed sympathetically. 'What will you do now, return to New York?'

Such a prospect no longer held any attraction for Gower. He had come to feel that he belonged out West. New York was now the past, and until recently Mercedes had been the future. Now it was as if his life was suspended. He had no trail to follow, as O'Neill would put it.

He shook his head slowly. 'I haven't given it much thought Liam. How did you come to follow me out here?'

'A combination of things, I suppose,' O'Neill replied. 'I spent a lot of time worrying about you and Ellie out here. Then they moved Captain William Caxton to Askaro Bend as the Officer Commanding. Me and him have been enemies since we served together way back. It became difficult for me, so I left to come out here. The trouble is that they'll work out where I am from what I told Mercedes.'

'What will happen if you go back, Liam?' an anxious Ellie enquired.

'I can't go back, Ellie. My army career ended the day I rode out of Askaro Bend, and my life will end if I ride back in.'

'You mean . . . ?' she began, unable to finish her question.

'I mean that I'm a deserter,' O'Neill said, 'and as such I will either be put to death by musketry or sent to prison for life.'

'If you can't go back, what will you do?'

Before replying to Ellie, O'Neill took a look out of the window. 'A thaw is beginning to set in, which means that I'll soon have to ride away from here before they send a party out to arrest me.'

This upset Ellie, and Gower warned O'Neill, 'It will be months before you are well enough to get back in the saddle, Liam. Try it before then and that hole in your chest will open up.'

'If the army comes for me they'll likely open up more than one hole in my chest,' O'Neill reminded him.

'They probably won't come,' Gower predicted.

His prophecy was proved false early on a morning ten days later, when Ellie called urgently to Gower, 'The hill!'

With the still very weak O'Neill asleep, Gower hurried to stand beside her at the window. A lopsided moon added little light to the dawn of a new day. It floated in the sky above the dark spruce-covered slope that slanted steeply upwards away from the cabin. At first he could see nothing, but he kept looking because he had learned to trust Ellie completely. Five horsemen were riding slowly out of the mist shrouding the upper rim. They came closer and closer down the slope, not bothering to use the screen of brush to conceal their advance. When they were a little nearer, Gower could see that they were in uniform.

'Soldiers!'

'Yes,' Ellie whispered, as if frightened that the distant riders would hear her. 'What do we do, Gerald?'

Reaching for his rifle, Gower said, 'Wake Liam carefully; don't alarm him. Tell him what's happening and that I said that I'll take care of this and he should lie still.'

When she had left his side, Gower raised his rifle to his shoulder and squinted along the sights. Not risking spoiling his aim by dwelling overlong in the aim, he fired a shot over the head of the lead rider.

There was no panic among the soldiers. A disciplined military team, they split to each side of the trail, taking cover first in the brush and then the trees. Gower waited for their next move, prepared to defend O'Neill to the last, while at the same time sombrely aware that he would be putting Ellie and her daughter at risk. Behind him he could hear O'Neill say something, his normally low voice reduced further in volume by weakness. Then a shout came from up in the trees.

'Are you there, Mr Gower? Gerald Gower?'

'I'm here,' Gower called back.

'This is Captain Caxton, United States Army, Mr Gower. I am here under orders from Thomas Durant of the Union Pacific Railway Company. Is the woman and child there with you?'

'They are here, Captain.'

'Are both unharmed?'

'They are both well.'

'And Lieutenant O'Neill?' Caxton called.

Making no answer, Gower looked behind him. O'Neill was sitting up in his bed, needing both of Ellie's arms round him for support. He appeared to be trying to swing his legs out on to the floor, but Ellie was struggling to prevent him from doing so. The baby girl, frightened by the sound of Gower firing his rifle, was moving around in her cot, crying loudly.

'I know that Lieutenant O'Neill is there with you, Gower,' Captain Caxton shouted. 'We are here to arrest that officer, and you would be unwise to obstruct the United States Army. Lay down your weapon, Mr Gower, we are coming down.'

There was movement on both sides of the trail. Watching soldiers moved into view, rifles at the ready as they waited for the captain to issue an order. Gower also waited for Caxton. When the captain stepped out from behind a tree, Gower squeezed the trigger of his rifle. Bark flew from the trunk of a tree just inches above Caxton's hat, and he jumped back behind the tree. The troopers also ran from sight. In the cabin behind him, O'Neill was struggling to get into his uniform.

Anger was discernible in Captain Caxton's voice when he shouted, 'I do not want the woman or child to come to harm, Gower, but the responsibility is yours. I will count to three. Before reaching that number I want to see you throw your rifle out of that window. One . . . two . . . three . . . '

The silence that followed Caxton's count was so deep it was unearthly. Then five rifles opened up from behind the trees. Hollering at Ellie to get down, Gower jerked to one side as bullets smacked against the outside wall and whistled in through the window. Hearing one ricochet off the rear inner wall of the cabin, he glimpsed Ellie getting her child out of the cot and protecting the girl with her body as they lay on the floor.

Coming to Gower at a crouch, O'Neill said, 'I'll draw them away, Gerald. Cover me while I make it to that tree. From there I can get to my horse in the barn.'

'You'll never make it,' Gower said, holding O'Neill's arm to prevent him moving.

'I will if you cover me.'

'I meant because of your condition,' Gower muttered.

Shaking free of Gower's grasp, O'Neill told him, 'I have to try. It's me that William Caxton is after, and I won't put Ellie and the baby at any more risk.'

With that, O'Neill went out of the door before Gower could stop him. Moving back into the window, Gower sent rapid fire up into the trees as from the corner of his eye he saw O'Neill running for the tree close to the cabin. Ellie had come to Gower's side and he heard her despairing cry.

'Oh, no!'

Gower saw O'Neill start up the little grass bank to the tree. His right foot slipped on a patch of thawed snow that had refrozen in the night. Trying to keep his balance, weakened by his wound, O'Neill fell, crashing heavily into the tree as he went down, O'Neill lay still, apart from the rapid rise and fall of his chest. He was safe from fire from up the slope, but Gower's skeleton turned to ice inside of him as he saw the dark stain spreading on the front of his tunic.

Ellie gasped as she saw it, too. 'Oh, dear God, Gerald, he'll bleed to death.'

That was true. From the knowledge he had gained when O'Neill had first been injured, Gower estimated that with his wound reopened, the lieutenant would last for no more than ten minutes.

'I'll have to go to him.'

Putting out an arm to bar Ellie's way as she spoke, Gower jerked them back from the window as a fusillade of shots came from up on the hill.

'You'd be dead before you got six feet,' he told her.

'But we can't leave him out there to die, Gerald.'

Starkly aware of this, Gower couldn't think of an alternative. Ellie was shaking and her daughter was screaming as bullets drummed against the front wall of the cabin. If he didn't do something soon, then they would all die.

He turned to Ellie. 'I want you to get back down on the floor, and keep your daughter safe. Promise me that you'll do that.'

'What are you going to do?' she asked, a tremor in her voice.

'Promise?' he gritted between clenched teeth.

'I promise.'

Satisfied by this, Gower got ready to take the only action open to him. He had to make a suicidal run at Caxton and his troopers, hoping to get enough of them to save Ellie, her baby and

O'Neill before they killed him. Firing fast from the window, he heard Ellie scream at him to come back as he plunged out of the door.

Firing his rifle as he went, he zigzagged towards the trees. Something hit him hard in the lower part of his right leg. Gower guessed it was a bullet, but it didn't impede him in any way. He heard a trooper shout, 'I'm hit, sir, hurt real bad.'

One down, four to go, Gower told himself, keeping tight behind the tree trunk as he reloaded his rifle for another rush at the riflemen on the hill. He dived into the open, doing a crouching run as he fired again and again. Bullets screamed by him while others ripped foliage apart on each side of him.

Then the firing stopped. Mystified, he dropped flat on the ground and looked up the hill. Four riders had come over the hill. His right leg bleeding now and giving him pain, Gower recognized one of the riders as

Mercedes. He was telling himself that he was hallucinating, but then he saw that her father was on the horse next to her. One of the other two horsemen was shouting something. Ears ringing from the rifle fire, Gower was then able to pick out the words.

'Stop, I say. Stop this nonsense at once.'

A shocked Gower identified the man who had shouted. He stood up, rifle under his arm. The man was Colonel Silas Seymour, whom Gower had last seen in New York. At Seymour's side was the outsized figure of Howland Yell. As Caxton and the troopers came out of the trees, the four riders sent their horses at a walk towards Gower. But he turned and did a limping run from them, heading for where O'Neill lay.

Ellie was already kneeling at the ashen-faced O'Neill's side, the remainder of the torn blanket in her hand. Ripping O'Neill's tunic open, Gower winced at the sight of blood pumping out fast. There was no time to sterilize the blanket. Quickly fashioning swabs from the blanket, Ellie cleared blood from the wound to get a clear view of how to plug the hole. Gower felt it was a waste of time, for O'Neill looked to be dead. But Ellie continued to work swiftly and deftly, plugging the wound and then co-operating with Gower as he tightly bandaged O'Neill's chest. Peering worriedly at the injured man's white face, Ellie bent to put her cheek close to his lips. The deep frown on her face slowly cleared and she managed a smile for Gower.

'He's breathing, Gerald.'

Both relieved, they stayed on their knees but looked up to see the four people looking down at them from the backs of their horses. Caxton, a tall, thin man, and his troopers were standing some distance away.

'I wouldn't have recognized you, Gerald,' Silas Seymour smiled down at him. 'You were a city gent the last time I saw you, now you are a frontiersman.'

'The transformation didn't come

easily,' Gower said cynically, not caring about anything now, except that Liam O'Neill lived.

'I think that the new image suits you,' Seymour said with a kindly smile.

Gower stood, and Ellie raised herself up at his side, pushing her mass of hair back from her face. Gower looked straight at Colonel Seymour. 'I suppose I should apologize for letting down the Union Pacific, sir.'

'On the contrary,' Seymour said, his face serious. 'Would you like to explain to Mr Gower, Howland?'

Nodding, Yell rested both arms on his saddle horn as he addressed Gower. 'We got ourselves off to a bad start, Gower, but I'm ready to admit that I made a mistake about you. You have proved yourself.'

'I don't understand.'

Samuel Glendon took over from Yell. 'What Mr Yell is saying, Gerald, is that your coming to the rescue of Mrs Mayne, the widow of a farmer, has convinced the farmers that this valley will be safe in the hands of the Union Pacific. Compromises on both sides will be necessary, but you have done more than we could have expected from any man, Gerald.'

'Does that mean that I still have a job?' Gower, both surprised and relieved, asked.

'My dear sir, a job for life if you wish,' Glendon replied, adding with a mischievous grin, 'Mercedes is quite looking forward to working with you again. In fairness, I should warn you that I suspect that she has more ambitious plans for you.'

Feeling able to do so then, Gower looked up at Mercedes for the first time. She was blushing, but gave him a sweet smile. Looking down at his leg, she said, 'You are hurt, Gerald.'

'It's nothing,' he smiled back at her, having forgotten the wound until she had mentioned it. Gower then looked down at O'Neill before asking Seymour. 'What will happen to Lieutenant O'Neill, sir?'

A serious-faced Seymour answered, 'Liam O'Neill will, of course, be hospitalized. When he is fully recovered, he will, due to his actions here . . . '

As the colonel paused, Gower exchanged glances with an anguished Ellie, then they both listened as Seymour continued ' . . . due to his actions here, Liam will be promoted to the rank of captain.'

Smiling happily, Ellie then dropped anxiously to her knees as O'Neill rattlingly cleared his throat. Fearing the worst, she clutched frantically at the injured man's hand. She jerked back in shock as he spoke hoarsely.

'Can a man afford to keep a wife and family on a captain's salary, sir?'

Filled with admiration for the tough O'Neill, who was holding tightly to Ellie's hand, Gower walked to stand by Mercedes' horse. He heard Silas Seymour speak jokingly.

'Do you have any particular lady in mind, Liam?'

We do hope that you have enjoyed reading this large print book.

Did you know that all of our titles are available for purchase?

We publish a wide range of high quality large print books including:
Romances, Mysteries, Classics
General Fiction
Non Fiction and Westerns

Special interest titles available in large print are:
The Little Oxford Dictionary
Music Book, Song Book
Hymn Book, Service Book

Also available from us courtesy of Oxford University Press:
Young Readers' Dictionary
(large print edition)
Young Readers' Thesaurus
(large print edition)

For further information or a free brochure, please contact us at:
Ulverscroft Large Print Books Ltd.,
The Green, Bradgate Road, Anstey,
Leicester, LE7 7FU, England.
Tel: (00 44) **0116 236 4325**
Fax: (00 44) **0116 234 0205**

STONE MOUNTAIN

Concho Bradley

The stage robbery had been accomplished by an old woman. Twine Fourch had never heard of a female being a highway robber before. He followed the trail all the way to a dilapidated log cabin up Stone Mountain. What happened after that no one could believe even after townsmen from Jefferson found the old log house and the skeletal dying old woman. But before the mystery could be solved there would be two unnecessary killings, a bizarre suicide and a lynching.

GUNS OF THE GAMBLER

M. Duggan

Destitute gambler Ben Crow arrives in Mallory keen to claim his inheritance, only to discover that rancher Edward Bacon has other ideas. Set up by Miss Dorothy, who had fooled him completely, Ben finds himself dangling on the end of a rope. Saved from death, Ben sets off in pursuit of Miss Dorothy, determined upon retribution. However, his quest for vengeance turns into a rescue mission when she is kidnapped by a crazy man-burning bandit.

97042